MW00811134

PJ Michaels is from Long Island, New York. He is a husband, father, and grandfather. He is also a musician, songwriter, and recording/live-performing artist. His passion for music was born when he had seen the Beatles perform on TV in 1964. After performing for many years, he met and married a beautiful woman; she had two young girls and he accepted them graciously as his own. Later they had a son together. With the children now grown-up and have families of their own, he has turned his talents to writing while still staying true to family and music.

To my beautiful wife, Donna, for withstanding the hours spent writing, re-writing, editing, and so on. I am grateful for her constant support, attitude, and encouragement to have me simply believe in myself and to keep moving forward. Thank you for all of that, Donna, I love you.

PJ Michaels

WHO'S LISTENING?

A HI-TECH, HIGH STAKES GAME OF ESPIONAGE AND MISTAKEN IDENTITIES

AUSTIN MACAULEY PUBLISHERS™

LONDON • CAMBRIDGE • NEW YORK • SHARJAH

Copyright © PJ Michaels (2021)

Ordering Information
Quantity sales: Special discounts are available on quantity purchases by corporations, associations, and others. For details, contact the publisher at the address below.

Publisher's Cataloging-in-Publication data
Michaels, PJ
Who's Listening?

ISBN 9781647503093 (Paperback)
ISBN 9781647503109 (Hardback)
ISBN 9781647503116 (ePub e-book)

Library of Congress Control Number: 2021909470

www.austinmacauley.com/us

First Published (2021)
Austin Macauley Publishers LLC
40 Wall Street, 33rd Floor, Suite 3302
New York, NY 10005
USA

mail-usa@austinmacauley.com
+1 (646) 5125767

I want to thank Austin Macauley publishing for this opportunity. My communications with Antonia, Ashley, Emily, Emma, Henry, and the entire production staff. Whether by phone or via email, have been outstanding. To my daughter-in-law, Kristin, thank you for your most invaluable input. Your feedback was instrumental in helping me bring this book to life, thank you. To those in the focus group: I want to thank all of you that took the time to read my manuscript and provide to me your thoughts and notes. All of this played a role in the completion of this work, so again, I thank you. With special thanks and gratitude to: Nirali S., Ashish S., Julia B., Samantha C., Pat L., Justin T., JT, Dan W., Jared S.

Introduction

With more and more people installing one or more voice-activated units in their homes, it will not be long until absolute privacy is outdated. Are you being listened to right now? In addition, do you know who is really listening?

Technology is great and it has introduced another new series of hi-tech servants for the home. The latest tech gadgets are listening devices, controlled by voice command. For the most part, it seems to be a great idea. You speak out and request music, news, or whatever you choose and it will play it for you. On the other hand, if you are just relaxing sitting on the sofa, calling out channels, or programs to the listening TV. It all seems pretty convenient, harmless, and safe. At least when the devices are used as *designed.*

Prologue

It begins – New York City – 2016: Ricky and Sara Rogers for all appearance's sake seem to be typical young, strong, and successful business professionals. They work and live in New York City. He handles commercial real estate and government real estate contracts for land acquisitions. Most of his transactions take place at his Park Avenue office and he is very successful. He is always dressed impeccably when working. He's around six feet tall, dark, almost black hair and stark blue eyes. Ricky always had the right color and style suit. Usually, he wore dark blue, black, or charcoal; he also has all of the dress shirts custom fitted to the contour of his lean, muscular frame. He wears only silk ties and a silk handkerchief in the breast pocket of the suit jacket. He always looks great. His style is almost a throwback to the 1950s or something, but it works for him. When he is not working, shorts and tee shirts are usually how you will find him, except of course during the winter months. Then it is either jeans and sweatshirts or full-on sweats. Sara works in mid-town. She is a very successful intellectual property lawyer. She too is always very well dressed. Sara has dark red hair and she keeps it long. She too is near six feet tall with sparkling green eyes, like cats' eyes, sharp and clear. When at work, she wears various designer outfits and business suits, she loves the colors green, black, navy, and tan. She is also outgoing, friendly, and nice to everyone. They appear to be a great couple truly living the 'American Dream.' This is the desired illusion. Ricky Rogers is originally from Westchester, NY. In 1996, at the age of 15, his family relocated to New York City. His father, Benjamin Rogers, is a very successful criminal defense attorney. His mother, Angela, was a stay-at-home mom. His father would, on occasion discuss a special case after its conclusion. He framed-out only the headlines and the results; win or lose. One case he spoke of was about getting a man cleared of all charges in an espionage case. Ricky, who barely listens to these stories, seemed to become quite interested in this subject. For some reason, the thought of the espionage game struck a chord within him. While his interest in the law was peaked at this point, it was the fantasy thought of being an international spy that stayed with him. He of course still had his first love of electronics and computers. Ricky attended only private schools, already being prepared for college. Sara McBride is originally from Long Island, N.Y. Her family moved to New York City in 1997. Her father, Avery McBride, is a Wall Street managing director. He too is very successful. Sara's mother, Barbara, donates her time at local soup kitchens helping to feed the homeless of New York City. Sara had witnessed the toll her father's job took on him every time there was a large dip in the stock market. During those periods he would come home from work looking beleaguered from dealing with all of the yelling clients as they were losing their investments and for some their life's savings. This was not something Sara had seen as a path she wanted to follow. Her interests from early on were in the law. Her favorite televisions shows were always about the law. She watched court dramas, trials, and the results. Intellectual property law was a subject she was most interested in. She had first read about it in a law magazine article one day, while she was having coffee at a local downtown village coffee bar/bookstore. Intellectual property law deals with the rules for securing and enforcing legal rights to inventions, designs, and artistic works. Practicing this avenue of the law caught her focus and she continued to follow that path and later pursue it further in college. After graduating high school in 2003, several colleges accepted Ricky. He chose to attend New York University, (NYU), for 2004 fall semester. Several colleges also accepted Sara and she too chose NYU to pursue her law degree. Ricky met Sara initially at a freshman welcome party held in the campus courtyard. Anyone looking on would have clearly seen a connection take place between Ricky and Sara when introduced by a couple of mutual friends. After they meet briefly, Sara explains, "Well, Ricky, it's nice to meet you. I am sorry but I have another event to attend. See ya' round the campus."

She smiles, turns, and walks away. There was a connection there but it did not fully reveal itself at this meeting.

The college years flew by even though the workload for both of them was very intense. Neither of them had the time to attend various social events. It was near the end of the spring semester of 2008. They had separately gone to one of the lecture halls to listen to an afternoon classical string concert. During the performance intermission, Ricky, and several others stepped outside to smoke or to get something to drink or eat from the five catering trucks set up outside the hall. Everything from big, soft, hot pretzels, to Philly-Cheese Steaks, hot dogs, gyros to falafel, they had it all. There is no food or beverage allowed in the lecture hall. Ricky was waiting on the beverage line. From behind, someone taps on his shoulder. He turns and sets his eyes on the most beautiful woman he has ever seen. Slowly realizing that he had met her somewhere before.

"Hi, reaching out to shake his hand, my name is Sara, Sara McBride and you are?"

"Hi Sara, I'm Ricky, Ricky Rogers. We met four years ago when we were freshman."

"You remembered that? It seems like so long ago. Well, it's nice to meet you again, Ricky Rogers."

"Nice to meet you again as well, Sara McBride. Are you on line to get a drink?"

"No, not really, I saw you inside the hall and you looked familiar. I just wanted to introduce myself. I hope you don't find me too forward."

Just then a bell began to ring from the lecture hall entrance, indicating that the concert was about to resume.

"Well, Sara, do you want to go back inside for the rest of the concert?"

"No, Beethoven is not really my thing, I prefer Mozart."

"I like some things from Beethoven but I do prefer Mozart as well and as this is not Mozart; do you want to take a walk?"

"Sure, let's take a walk over to Washington Square Park."

"What are you studying, Sara?"

"I'm studying law."

"What area of the law are you most interested in?"

"Well, for the most part, it has been general studies and various types of cases and their outcomes. I want to focus on becoming an intellectual property lawyer right here in good old New York City. And you, what are you studying, Ricky?"

"I'm studying computer science and electronics engineering."

"They sound like pretty tough courses."

"Well, yes, but I'm not studying law, that must be tough too."

"It is, and I think it will be worth it."

Ricky and Sara continued to see each other initially just casually dating. Their relationship began overtime to strengthen and grow. At some point shortly after graduation, they both began their careers. A law firm in the midtown area had hired Sara as an intellectual property lawyer. As for Ricky, he receives an invitation to a cocktail party from one of his father's friends. He decided to accept the invitation. At the gathering he is introduced to a group of high-end real estate brokers as Ben Rogers's son. While this decision to attend was a departure from his field of study, he took to it like a fish to water. He became involved heavily in real estate, commercial real estate.

Ricky and Sara decide to take an apartment together. The apartment they wanted, did not allow singles so they signed the lease as Ricky and Sara Rogers. They have now been together for eight years. Their collective past is not what you would think based on what you see. Ricky and

Sara and their inside operative at the department of defense, John Klegman, are all third-generation Americans. Americans, but they are all homegrown Russian spies. They all attended American schools and colleges. One day during his senior year in college, Ricky's father called and asked him to bring some papers he left at home and needs them for an appointment that afternoon. Ricky hailed a cab, went to his parents' apartment, retrieved the papers, and then took the cab to the office. There he meets the man his father had cleared on espionage charges years earlier. His father introduced him to Alex Zeblonsky. They were working on another case. During the 'small talk' conversation, Alex learns from Ricky's father, that he is attending NYU, and of Ricky's prowess with computers and electronics. Ricky hands the papers to his father, excuses himself and leaves the office to return to the campus. Several days later, Ricky was walking across the campus grounds when he is approached by a man. The man introduces himself only as 'Eagle.' He is over six feet tall, bald and he wore a green and black tee-shirt, jeans and dark wraparound sunglasses. He tells Ricky that Alex, the man his father saved in court, told him to make contact. Eagle asked Ricky if he was interested in espionage.

Ricky looks him the eye. "Who are you? Eagle? Who sent you?"

"Look, I told you, Alex asked me to find you. He said it's easy work and there is a lot of money to be made. He said you would be a good one, take this."

Eagle gives him a business card with nothing on it but a handwritten phone number.

"A good one, what do you mean a good one?"

"Hey, just call the number, and oh yeah, I was never here."

He turns and quickly but confidently walks away and disappears out of sight. Ricky finds Sara and tells her about this encounter and she too was intrigued. Ricky calls the number and he mentions that he works in tandem with a partner. He asked that both be allowed to attend. They are both welcome. He accepts the invitation to the meeting. At that meeting, they meet, Ivan. The man Ricky had spoken with earlier on the campus grounds was a younger man, early 40s. Ivan was an older man. A tall, thin man with a full head of grey hair kept just longer than a full military haircut, and a large well-groomed white mustache. He explained why they were there. They meet another person, John Klegman. John was tall, just less than six feet, in good shape, light brown hair with dark brown eyes. He too was dressed in jeans wearing a dark blue tee-shirt. This was their introduction to the KGB. They attended many late-night classes, night classes conducted by the KGB. They accepted their first mission. They are to acquire U.S. satellite transmission codes. Ricky designs an electronic device, a signal receiver. It can capture any type of digital transmission. On an early Saturday morning, Ricky and Sara go to Penn Station and take the Long Island Rail Road out to Montauk Point, Long Island. They spent the afternoon walking around the town. They visited some of the small, boutique shops. They had lunch at a local eatery and then made their way to the beach. After viewing a beautiful red and orange sunset, it became a clear night, with gentle breezes coming in off the ocean. He sets his equipment up on a platform that he unfolds. He turns the unit on and covers the screen with a blanket so he will not attract attention. The captured data streams into a computer program that Ricky created. The program collects the data and performs the analysis. Ricky then scans the data and extracts what he needs to deliver. They stayed the night in an ocean view hotel in Montauk. They caught the 10:10 a.m. train back to Manhattan on Sunday. Later that day, Ricky and Sara go to meet with Ivan to deliver the information. Ivan is seated in a high-back, black leather office chair behind a beautiful, somewhat ornate, maple-colored, antique desk and he reviews the information. He looks at Ricky and smiles.

"You did good, Ricky, very good indeed."

He reaches down under his desk and brings up a light grey briefcase. He hands it to Ricky. "Here, take this, this is yours, you earned it."

"Thank you very much, Ivan, do you need anything else?"

"No, that is it, now go and finish your college. Except for one thing, are you not curious as to the contents in the briefcase I handed you?"

"Actually, no sir, you had explained the arrangement very clearly, and I believe you to be a man of your word. So, with all due respect, Ivan, I am sure the contents are as agreed. Once again, thank you, Ivan. Well, I have some other tasks to attend to so, if there is nothing else…"

"No Ricky, you can go. Go and take care of your other tasks. We may speak again sometime. I am going to recommend both of you for a future assignment. At some point you will be hearing from another man known only as the captain, do as he says, and be well."

Ricky and Sara left and returned to NYU to complete their courses and graduate. It was an exciting time for both of them.

Neither of them ever spoke of the compensation they received. As per the agreement, they were paid 500,000 dollars, in cash. Sara has a private storage space in her parents' apartment building. They took a cab to the apartment building and went into the storage area. They only took 300 dollars each out of the briefcase then they placed the briefcase inside and locked the storage unit. They walked partway back to NYU when it started to rain. They jumped into the first cab that would stop for them to complete the trip back to the campus.

Chapter 1

On a sunny Sunday June morning, Ricky is sitting at the mahogany oval kitchen table, reading the newspaper, and enjoying a hot cup of coffee. When he hears his encoded phone beeping that he had a message. He gets up and goes into the bedroom to get his phone. He accesses the voicemail and listens to the message, "Hello, Ricky, this is the captain. Meet me at Chelsea Pier at five p.m. today."

There was no caller I.D. Ricky goes into the living room to tell Sara, "I received a message from the captain; you know the one Ivan said would call at some point. We are to meet him this afternoon at Chelsea Pier at five p.m."

"The captain, did he say why?"

"No, he just said for us to meet him there. I will call a car service to bring us downtown to the pier."

It was a beautiful warm afternoon, a great time to be down at the pier. While they are walking and talking and having iced cocktails. They were enjoying the beautiful day, and the waterfront scenery. Several colorful sailboats and other assorted powered boats, as well as some rather large barges and various cruise ships. You can see the massive barges making their way into the harbor escorted by three red tugboats, each with black sides and bottoms. At one point while Ricky and Sara are just walking around the pier, a man approaches them. He is a large muscular figure over six feet tall, and appears to be in his early 50s, wearing jeans, and a dark blue tee-shirt carrying a thin black briefcase. He has jet-black hair with silver temple streaks and dark aviator-style sunglasses. He introduces himself to them as simply as the captain. They understood who he was; they walked off to a quieter area of the pier. The captain explained the mission to them and told them where they were to report for updates on progress and successful completion. What they did not know was the FBI was following this man and taking as many photographs as they can whenever he appears, which is rare. Those photographs now also have Ricky and Sara even though they did not realize at the time. The latest round of photos, capture them speaking in a somewhat secluded area of the pier with the man known only as 'the captain.' It did not take long for the FBI to identify Ricky and Sara from the photographs. They requested a computer search after an image scan. They identified him as Ricky Rogers, and she was found to be Sara McBride. They found out that Ricky and Sara reside in the Riverside Park Luxury Apartments at Riverside Drive and 79th street, New York. They are living there as Ricky and Sara Rogers. They immediately place a request for joint surveillance teams with the NYPD and FBI to be set up across the street from their building. Two agents went to Ricky and Sara's building.

With the building manager, Sal Catania, they went to each apartment to ask the tenants as a matter of national security, would they consider taking an all-expense-paid luxury vacation and allowing them the use of their apartment. Surprisingly, all the tenants decline the offer. With only one floor left, they went up to the tenth floor. Sal knocks on the door. "Hey, Sam, it's Sal Catania, some people from the FBI are here to see you."

The apartment door opens and an elderly, six-foot-tall and powerfully built grey-haired man answers, "Can I help you?"

"Yes sir, I am Agent Philips and this is Agent Guarino with the FBI, are you Mr. Sam Elliston?"

"Yes, I am, sir."

"Mr. Elliston, your country needs you right now. Actually, it needs your apartment may we speak with you about it?"

He was former military and so he let them in the apartment. Sal went back down to his office.

"Okay gentlemen, have a seat, now, what's this all about? Oh, excuse me; this is my wife, Arlene. Arlene, these are agents Philips and Guarino from the FBI."

Arlene is about five-feet-four, her hair is white and she keeps a short-cropped hairstyle. She too is still in great shape.

"The FBI, what do you want with us," she asks?

"It's nice to meet you, Mrs. Elliston; we need this apartment for surveillance. We're authorized to give you an all-expense-paid vacation, full luxury treatment, and 10,000 dollars in cash for you to use on that vacation or any way you like. We will also subsidize the rent for as long as we use the apartment in exchange for allowing us to use this space for two, maybe three weeks. It would be no more than a month for sure. So, what do you think, Mr. and Mrs. Elliston?"

Sam gets up slowly from his brown saddle leather recliner and asks for a moment with his wife in private. The agents agree. Sam and Arlene go into the den and return after five minutes or so. "Gentlemen, I believe we have a deal."

Sam reaches out to shake hands when Arlene then steps forward to Agent Philips, blocking the handshake, and then whispers in the agent's ear, "Europe and we have a deal."

Agent Philips smiles and takes out his phone. He makes all of the arrangements on the spot and the couple left the next morning. A limousine picked them up at 8 a.m. and drove them to LaGuardia Airport in Queens, NY. The agents arrived shortly after the limousine left and installed the new 'tenants.' They moved in two agents, a man and a woman posing as Al and Alice Albright. They moved to New York ten years ago from Ohio as their back-story. Their assignment is to be friendly, as so-called 'out-of-towners.' They need to get close to Ricky and Sara to see what they can learn about them. The FBI knows of this man, 'the captain' but he has not done anything yet as far as they know. Right now, all they can do is watch. Their nickname within the squad is simply, 'the Watchers.' There were several FBI agents stationed at various known sighting checkpoints in the downtown area. No matter how hard they try, the captain always seems to elude their surveillance and returns to his basement command center undetected. He will generally wait until sundown to make his way back. He walks through the streets of downtown and the agents begin to follow about one block behind him. The captain slips into a maze of old, rundown, abandoned apartments. He steps inside a certain building and immediately goes down into the basement. The trailing agents lose him. It is completely dark in this basement and there are piles of debris. Old mattresses, old broken furniture, out of use old boilers, and brown corrugated storage boxes piled to the ceiling, wherever that may be because you cannot see anything in the dark. If you don't know your way, you will not get through it and you may not even be able to find your way back out should you try to follow, if you knew where he went. The captain makes his way quietly through the dangerous maze of invisible hazards and exits out the fire safety window on the other side of the basement. He slowly sticks his head out of the window and looks around before sliding out through the window into a narrow, shadow-filled alley and then he walks around to the back-basement entrance that leads to his command center. He has met with his agents. They know the mission. He will wait with his comrades for the first report on their progress.

Chapter 2

Ricky and Sara live in an apartment building on the upper west side near Riverside Park, which is simply incredible. It is a huge apartment on the 11th floor, and it spans the entire space. All of the residences in this building are the entire floor. Their apartment of course; is very nicely decorated with the finest furnishings. There are large windows in the apartment that go from the floor to the ceiling on the west side of the apartment. The windows allow lots of light and offer great views of Riverside Park. It is private because there are no other apartments on the floor just theirs. They have barely become acquainted or generally interact with anyone in the building. There is one exception though and that is with the neighbor's one floor down, Al and Alice Albright. Al is an accountant. He stands just less than six feet tall. He has light brown hair that he keeps short. He has hazel eyes and wears round, transient shaded eyeglasses with a thin black frame. No matter what the event you will always find Al with a white dress shirt, khaki pants, a bow tie, and glasses. Even at a picnic in Central Park, it did not matter, that was Al. Alice, on the other hand, is a clothing designer. She is five-foot-eight inches tall and appears to be in great shape. She has dark brown, luminous eyes. When she looks at you, eye to eye, you can see sparks of light flash in her eyes. She has long blonde hair that reaches the upper middle of her back and falls over her shoulders. Most of the time; you will find her wearing jeans, ankle boots, and a simple top. That is unless there's a fashion show in town on the calendar, then it's business casual all the way. When a show is scheduled, she will put on extra help for preparation, arranging the sequencing for the fashion creations, and music for the show. She makes calls from her home office to line up all of the models she wants to wear her creations. Alice always registers to participate in fashion shows. She generally does very well at these shows. She typically gets several orders for her upcoming line of new fashion styles.

The sales come from buyers at the show and post-show sales from her website. Al and Alice have come a long way since they left their home in Ohio and decided to move to New York. Though they had left Ohio and moved to New York ten years prior, they were still for the most part true Midwesterners. When Al and Alice first meet Ricky and Sara, it was a Tuesday evening after work. They met in the apartment building lobby. While they were waiting for the elevator Al started a little small talk conversation, like, "Beautiful day today, wouldn't you say?"

The four struck up a brief conversation when Al suggests, "Hey, why don't we grab a booth in the piano lounge and have some drinks?"

Ricky looks at Sara. "Would you like to join them?"

"Sure, let's go."

They walk into the lounge; it is dark and not very crowded. They find a booth near the piano player. He was performing some standards like, *'Fly Me to the Moon.'* *'Stardust'* and several numbers made most popular by Frank Sinatra. *'Luck Be a Lady,'* *'My Way,'* *'Chicago,'* and of course, *'New York, New York.'* The waiter comes over and introduces himself, "Good evening, my name is Raphael. Would any of you care for anything from the bar?"

Sara tells the waiter, "I will have a Grey Goose chocolate martini."

Alice contemplates the beverage options then tells the waiter, "That sounds good, make it two."

Raphael then turns to the men, "Excuse me, would you gentlemen care for anything from the bar?"

Ricky orders, "I'll have a gentleman Jack Daniels with ice."

"Thank you and you, sir?"

"I will have Grey Goose vodka on the rocks."

"Thank you, I will be back with your order shortly." While they are waiting for their drinks, they resume their conversations.

Al tells them, "Yeah, we just bought one of those new auto-listening devices, my first one. Do you guys have one?"

"Yes Al, we do have one, and I love it," Sara tells them.

"You just call out a command like, play soft music, and just like that, the music begins to play."

"We can't wait to hook ours up and check it out," said Alice.

Al turns to Ricky, "So, Ricky, what do you do for a living?"

"I handle large commercial real estate transactions. I also handle government land site surveys and land acquisitions. What about you, Al, what is it you do?"

"Me?"

"I am a CPA, you know, a certified public accountant."

"Yes Al, I know the term CPA. Do you like that type of work?"

"Yes I do, and do you know why, Ricky?"

"Well, no, not really."

"It's simple, you see Ricky, numbers don't lie. People can lie, but not numbers."

"Oh, yes, I see. Well, you know what they say."

"No, what do they say Ricky?"

"They say if you love what you do you will never have to work a day in your life."

"Really, well, that must be so because it has never felt like work to me."

"Hey, here is the waiter with our drinks. Yeah, Alice and I both work downtown, near the Chelsea Pier. We are usually done with work around four-thirty. If we do not go to the pier, we are usually home by five-thirty. Alice and I like to go to the pier after work sometimes and have a couple of drinks to unwind after a long day before we head back uptown. Alice has a nice office in our place too. She set it up in one of the smaller bedrooms on the west side with those large windows. She sometimes works from home to handle her fashion business. So, where are you from originally, Ricky?"

Ricky is not one that is generally fazed by a question coming out of leftfield but he froze at this question. He quickly looks at Sara and then looks back at Al. "The Midwest."

"No kidding; we're from the Midwest too, Ohio. What part of the Midwest are you from, Ricky?"

Ricky again darts his eyes to Sara and then he turns to Al saying, "Hey, oh, look at the time, I'm so sorry, I forgot to get a few items from the store earlier. We need to get there before they close. Would you please excuse us?"

Ricky takes out his two-tone, black/charcoal grey leather wallet to pay for the drinks and Al puts his hand up and stops him.

"Sure, no problem Ricky, put your wallet away, we got this. We'll see you both again soon."

With that, Ricky and Sara make their way out of the piano bar and through the lobby to tend to the 'forgotten' errands. Al and Alice finish their drinks and get the elevator to head upstairs and home. Ricky and Sara exit the building, she asks him, "Hey, what just happened in there, everything was going well I thought?"

"I don't know, for some reason when Al asked me, 'So, where are you from originally, Ricky?' I froze. There was something about his voice when he said it. Then when he asked where in the Midwest, he sounded like Al again, I just blanked."

"You blanked, what do you mean you blanked? You know the Midwest cover is always Wichita Kansas."

"Yes, I know, I just froze. I don't why, so I had to get out of there. Besides, we do need to report to our superior officer."

Chapter 3

The superior officer on this mission is Captain Ben Yurjinsky. He and his men are set up in a dark basement office in an old apartment building downtown. "Yes Ricky, we should go now and get it over with."

"Yes, I agree."

They quickly walk up a few blocks and go around the corner at 76th street, out of sight from the tenth-floor vantage point of Al and Alice just in case for some reason they happened to be looking out the windows.

Ricky was spooked for some reason by Al's inquiry about where they were from and he was not sure why. They hail a cab and tell the driver to bring them downtown to Washington Square Park. They tell the driver to drop them off near the Arch. When they arrive, he pays the driver in cash and they begin walking again. The address they were given, 999 Bleeker Street, is several blocks away. It is an old, run-down, tattered, red brick apartment building. They do not go in. They stand near the main front entrance just looking at this old, poorly lit, building for a few moments. Then they turn around and start to walk back in the direction they had just come from. Walking back up the block a bit, they reach the side of the building and they slowly make their way down a light-less flight of metal stairs. At the bottom of the stairs was a door and through the door they faintly hear yelling, yelling in a foreign language. Ricky knocks on the door. As the door opens slightly, he tries to peer inside. The men in the room are armed with AK47 assault rifles, shotguns, and nine-millimeter side arms. They were all dressed alike. Dark green short sleeve collared shirts with a three-inch diameter, black outlined, circular patch on the breast pocket. The image on the patch was that of a spotted Eagle with what appears to be large prey clutched in its powerful talons. As soon as those inside the room realize that it is Ricky and Sara, they lowered their weapons. Captain Ben Yurjinsky was the lead man in the room, a steely-eyed, no-nonsense veteran.

"So, tell me, Ricky, how is your progress on the mission you were assigned?"

"I have been keeping in touch with John as often as I can. He is not always available. The last time we spoke he told me he is still collecting and compiling the data."

When Ricky finishes his report, the captain admonishes him for performing poorly. "You are wasting my time. You tell John I want the information now! The United States is currently in possession of new software that works in conjunction with its newly developed laser weapon. It is not just a laser. It is an incredibly powerful laser but of course, that is not all.

"The Americans have figured out a way to transmit data within the laser. Let us say we were to launch a missile toward a U.S. target, their satellites will undoubtedly detect the launch. The data that is collected streams to an antenna field somewhere in the U.S. The data is then loaded into their computers, and this new software allows them to encode whatever data they want. Do you understand?"

Ricky looks at Sara then back at him, they both shake their heads, no. "You know that a laser beam is faster than any missile, and its range can be limitless. They can lock onto a missile or an aircraft, fire their laser and it can destroy it or worse, with the data they can transmit they can change the coordinates. They could turn a jet bomber around and have it drop its ordinance on a target of their choice! Alternatively, they can send a missile back where it came from. Do you understand now?"

They both nod affirmatively then Ricky tells the captain, "I am sure John is working as quickly as possible. I will remain in contact with him daily and we will work out the details for the hand-off."

Then the captain looks at the both of them very seriously, "We need to ensure the safety of our country against a United States missile attack. Or for that matter, even one of our own."

He again speaks to Ricky, in Russian, "If your results are no different at our next meeting, I will be very disappointed. You will be effectively retired, both of you. So, go now and complete your mission. The clock is ticking."

Ricky now speaks to the captain in Russian, "I believe we are being too closely watched and this is greatly hampering our efforts, sir."

"Is there anyone in your building you can set up as a decoy?"

"Earlier this evening, we were having drinks with two neighbors in our building. They are from Ohio, maybe them."

The captain thinks for a moment, he looks at Ricky and still speaking in Russian, "These neighbors, do you think they can be played?"

"Yes."

"Ricky, listen to me, these neighbors may work to our advantage. You must find a way to cast suspicion on them. Whatever you decide to do, you need to do it covertly. They cannot know what is taking place. If you do this correctly, the surveillance team will begin to track and follow them. When this happens, you will be able to fulfill your orders and bring me what I seek. Now go!"

Ricky and Sara leave the meeting grateful to be alive. They also know now that the pressure is on. The operative inside the department of defense is John Klegman. He is a Sr. data analyst. He is covertly trying to acquire and compile the secret data when he can. Then somehow get the data to Ricky and Sara. The problem is, this is a secret defense area and the personnel are not allowed to leave the premises, they live at the facility, and no unauthorized personnel are allowed in. John has to walk out to the quiet area by the back-fence line near the large, wooded area just beyond. This is the only area where he can see some nature. He also gets the strongest phone signal in this area to communicate with Ricky. He gets a signal in the building but sometimes the calls drop. He uses his special issue cell phone. Ricky has the same. It is an encrypted phone so if anyone tries to listen in on their conversation, they will only hear garbled noise.

John calls Ricky and tells him, "I am very close to acquiring all of the data. We need to figure out a way for me to hand it off to you Ricky."

"I cannot even arrange a meeting with you because I am being watched."

"Watched, by whom?"

"I'm not sure John, NYPD, CIA, FBI, or KGB? This being New York City it is probably all of them. I will figure something out; we'll be in touch."

He finishes the phone call with John. He sits down at the kitchen table with a pad and pencil and begins scribbling out possible ways he can implicate his neighbors. He needs to shift the surveillance focus to the neighbors without them knowing it. This has to take place to allow him to complete this mission and in doing so, hopefully keeping both he and Sara alive and get the payoff. The next day, Wednesday, Ricky gets a call inviting him to a government office downtown to discuss some possible land acquisitions. He learns at the meeting that one of the sites is adjacent to his operative's location. *Perfect!* He thought to himself. He accepted the assignment and he will review the sites. He needs to call their office to schedule the walk-through dates. The meeting concludes and he makes his way home. He of course, was only interested in one piece of land next to the secured facility. Ricky knows of this property. It is currently a city-owned property held in a legal dispute. The property is secured by a seven-foot-high fence and a wired mesh covering that produces a silent alarm to the police if there is a break in the mesh of four inches or more throughout the entire surface area of the fence. The only access point is a locked main gate with a heavy chain and padlock. You need permission from the city to gain access. An appointment needs to be scheduled and an official escort is required to access and walk the property. When Sara comes home from work, Ricky tells her what took place at the meeting.

He looks at her smiling. "Sara, a big piece of the equation has just fallen into place. And I think I may know of a way to draw attention to the neighbors."

"Do you have a plan?"

"Yes, well, at least I think I do."

"What are you going to do?"

"First, we need to get closer to them. Maybe a casual visit, or go out for dinner. You know, to get a little better acquainted, yes that is the first step."

"Why Ricky? We do not get better acquainted with anyone, why them?"

"We need to get closer to them; do you remember the conversation we had with the captain? He asked me to set them up as decoys remember. Getting close to them is crucial for me to carry out my plan and implicate them."

"I don't understand where you are going with this."

Ricky has an ever so slight smile break across his face. His real estate endeavors and such are a front. He is, in his own right, a super electronics engineer, and a computer genius. They sit down on the black leather sofa in the den, and Ricky begins to lay out his plan to her.

"I took notice one day while sitting at the kitchen table. I called out to the listening device to play some jazz. Like magic, the music began to play and I went into a kind of a trance. At that exact moment I realized, that's it, I have it!!"

"Have what?"

"I know how I can divert the attention of those watching us."

"Okay, how?"

"Do you remember when we were talking with them that evening waiting into the lobby piano bar? We went in and had some drinks?"

"Yes, I remember, what about it?"

"Do you remember Al telling us he just bought a new auto-listening device?"

"Yes, he was going on about it for a bit, Alice too, so?"

"So?"

"So, we need to get closer to them. We need to get into their apartment somehow and we need to do it soon."

"How exactly are we going to do that?"

"I don't know how yet."

"And why do we need to get into their apartment?"

"I know how to modify these electronic units in several ways."

"So?"

"Wait a minute, Sara, let me tell you. I can modify these units to do whatever I want."

"Every unit has a small processor inside."

"I can modify its code and capture the devices I.D., its transmission I.D."

Sara, now listening intently tells him to, "Please continue."

"All of our devices today, the TV, cell phones, and the other listening devices transmit a code when called into action. The transmission carries an I.D. number that ties it to the owner of the unit that broadcasts the voice command. The authorities can listen and trace these devices if they have reasonable cause. By getting into their apartment I can access their machine, get the data I need and I'm done?"

"Done, what did you do?"

"With the data from their unit I can modify our unit. I can use a very special adapter and I can create a second SIM card and encode it with their data. Then I can program the cards to respond to English and transmit our I.D. to those that are listening. When we speak in Russian, it will transmit their I.D. We just make up some story about some crime or subversive activity like a kidnapping or a murder, as a decoy. Whatever we want it to be. Only when we speak of this as a conversation we must speak in Russian. All of sudden the watchers will be watching them not us. What do you think?"

Sara looks at him and smiles. "We need to get into that apartment."

The next day, Thursday, Ricky calls his office to rearrange his day's schedule. He pushes the late appointments to the next day because he needs the time to put his plan into action. Around nine-thirty in the morning, he takes the elevator down to the lobby. He goes out and down the street for a cup of coffee. He returns to the building and rings for the elevator. He goes to the ninth floor. He steps out of the elevator and walks around; all is quiet. He walks toward the end of the hall to a stairwell. He has another look around then enters the stairwell. He goes up the stairs to the tenth floor. He remembers Al saying they worked downtown when they were talking in the lobby piano bar and they are usually home by five-thirty. He also knows that Alice sometimes needs to work from home. She needs a quiet area to take care of the business side of the fashion business.

She will return phone calls and update the computer and other things she cannot do at her downtown location. Therefore, by this hour of the day, if you were going into your office you would already be there. Ricky continues to climb up the stairs.

Chapter 4

The building is still very quiet. Like everyone has gone off to work. He hopes that Alice is not working from home today. He gets to the landing on the tenth floor. He quietly opens the stairwell door ever so slightly just enough to get a glimpse down the hall to see if anyone was around. It all seemed quite still. He decided it was okay to proceed and he pushes open the door and right then the bell on the elevator sounds. He retreats into the stairwell quickly but quietly closing the door. He turns around to see the elevator's passengers. It was Alice; she was home. He sinks to the floor in the stairwell and he was hoping she did not see him. He thought about calling it off even though he knows what is at stake if he fails. He collects himself; cracks open the door. The hallway is empty, and she has gone into her apartment. He needs only a few minutes to rig one of his thin-body wireless HD cameras in a somewhat hidden location. The camera needs full view of the hallway and their apartment door. He needs to start learning their patterns. He begins to scout for the perfect place for his camera. He notices a large fire extinguisher mounted on the wall near the stairwell. He's about to set it in place when he hears the apartment door open. Once again, he spins around, opens the door, and ducks inside the stairwell. This time you could hear the door close. Alice was leaving and as she was locking the apartment door, she heard something; she heard the stairwell door close. It has a loud, very distinctive 'click' sound when it latches. Alice slowly walks across the hall to the elevator and reached to press the call button, but she freezes. She felt like someone was watching her. She does not call for the elevator; instead, she begins walking down the hallway toward the stairwell. With each step, her heart begins to beat a little faster.

She notices her hands were beginning to tremble a little. She cautiously approaches the stairwell door and from a distance, she peers through the glass. There was no one there but she still felt eyes on her. She thought for a moment, and then she walked right up to the glass door panel, pulled her hands up around the sides of her eyes, and stared right into the stairwell, nothing. Then she grabbed the handle and pulled the door wide open. She screams when she does this as a defense mechanism to scare them off. No one was there. With that, she closed the door and began walking back to the elevator. She thought for a moment and began to laugh at herself. She heard a sound and her imagination just took off. She called for the elevator and left. Ricky had gone back down the stairs almost back to the ninth floor. He heard Alice scream; he did not know why. He also heard the door close. He resumed his climb back up and re-entered the tenth floor. He mounts the camera to the wall near the fire extinguisher. Then he tests it out with the app on his phone. All of the functions work perfectly and the angle was great. The view captured the entire hallway. From their apartment door clear across to the elevator. He wipes down the door and the handles like he had wiped down the handrails in the stairwell. He looks and there is no one around so he walks toward the elevator. *No more stairs,* he thought. So, he takes the elevator back up to his apartment and collapses onto the plush, pillowed, light grey sofa in the living room. After a few moments, he gets up and goes into the kitchen to make a cup of coffee. He turns on his phone and opens the camera app. The camera captures the date, time, and frame rate data. All of the images are automatically transmitted in real-time to a secret server bank that Ricky has full access to through his specially encoded cell phone. The camera has a setting for motion-activation recording. It will automatically activate the camera when there is any motion in the hallway. This feature is used so the camera does not record hours of an empty hallway. Anytime the camera activates it sends a notification to his phone with the view on the screen. He left this camera in place for several days.

Ricky watched some of the activity live but mostly he studied the replays for their timing and patterns. The better he understands their rhythm the easier it will be to arrange a chance meeting. He notices from watching the replays that Al and Alice go to dinner most nights around seven p.m. Friday is a regular workday for both of them. Sara is in her office finishing up the week's work and planning out the next week. Ricky has several appointments today due to shifting his schedule around. After work, they are going out to a party in the Hampton's for the weekend. Monday rolls around and they again return to work.

Around four-thirty in the afternoon, Ricky calls Sara, "Hello?"

"Hi, Sara, I need you to be outside the building by six-forty-five this evening."

"Okay sure, why?"

"Because we are taking Al and Alice to dinner, they just don't know it yet. I'll see you outside the building at six-forty-five, be ready to hail a cab."

Sara arrives promptly at the scheduled time. She was dressed for a night on the town in a fitted forest green cocktail dress, black Chiku Pump stiletto's, small black and silver Prada cocktail purse, and a black shawl with an area across the back with ultra-fine, iridescent threads sewn in. They appear only as a shimmer for the most part. When the shawl catches the light just so, the iridescent threads form a heart. Ricky walks out of the building just as Sara arrives. He is wearing a dark grey suit, light gray shirt, and a simple, long black tie. The camera was still in place on the tenth-floor hallway and his cell phone receives a notification. He checks the phone and like clockwork, Al and Alice were getting into the elevator to go out for dinner. Ricky has Sara stand near the curb to hail a cab on his signal. He goes back into the building and waits in the lobby near the front door. He had a view of the elevator so he could watch its descent until it reached the lobby.

When the elevator reaches the main floor, Ricky waits just a couple of seconds and then makes his way out the door. He goes out of the building but he stops just a few paces in front of the entrance. He is supposedly looking for Sara. Al and Alice exit the building and find him standing there.

"Well, hello there Ricky," Al said, reaching out to shake hands.

Alice said hello as well, when Al asks, "Are you waiting for someone?"

"No, actually, I am looking for Sara. Oh, there she is," he calls out, "Sara! There she is right over there, she's hailing a cab, come on, come over and say hello."

Walking toward Sara, Ricky speaks to Al and Alice, "You know I never had a chance to apologize."

"Apologize?" Al asks. "What are you apologizing for?"

"Do you remember the first night we met?"

"Yeah, we were waiting for the elevator with you and Sara. We went into the piano bar for some drinks. Then right in the middle of the conversation, you had to run off somewhere."

"Yes," Ricky said, "That's what I'm talking about. I felt bad about that since that night because of my rudeness to you and Alice."

They both look at each other and then to Ricky, "Oh, nonsense, no harm, no foul, Ricky."

He is taken aback by their attitude but he needs to persist. "Thank you both so much for your understanding. I appreciate it and I insist that you join me and Sara for dinner tonight my treat, anywhere you want to go. It's just my way of saying thank you."

They were reluctant to accept at first, Al speaks with Alice for a moment and they agree to go. "Okay Ricky, why not, we accept."

"Great, look, Sara got us a cab, let's go to dinner."

The four go off to dinner and Ricky's plan seems to be unfolding as designed. They have a great time having dinner at 'Tavern on the Green.'

After dinner, it was still early and it was a beautiful early summer evening. They decide to take a walk around the streets of Manhattan followed by an impromptu stop at a popular local Irish pub for a nightcap.

Al and Alice tell Ricky and Sara they are going to be out of town for a few days, just a little break in the action. Al speaks to Ricky and Sara.

"I know we don't know each other all that well, we don't have any friends close by or family around and I do hate to impose."

"No problem Al, what do you need," Ricky asks.

"Well, okay, I hate to impose but would you consider watering the plants in our apartment a couple of times while we're gone?"

Ricky looks at Sara; she smiles. "Sure, it's okay with me."

Ricky turns back to Al, "Sure Al, sure, we will do that for you and Alice. When will you be leaving?"

"Wednesday, the day after tomorrow, we'll be back in three days, five the most. I will have another key made for you in the morning and I'll drop it into your mailbox, is that okay?"

"That will be fine, Al. Hey, it's getting late; I'm going to go pay for the drinks and get us a cab."

Before he goes to pay, Ricky turns and raises his glass. "I would like to propose a toast, to Al and Alice, enjoy your time off. We will take very good care of your plants, Cheers."

The others stood up and they brought their glasses together and then, bottoms up. They all share a cab back to the apartment. Alice tells Sara about the plants they have, and how best to tend to them. Sara tells her, "I love plants and flowers. Please tell me what I need to know."

They all seemed to be getting along quite well during the ride. Except maybe Ricky, you see while Alice and Sara were talking plants and flowers, Al was explaining a variety of accounting mishaps and all the things he needs to do to sort it out daily. Ricky just kind of sat there trying desperately to appear even a little interested in the cascade of numbers, equations, formulas, and mathematical mishaps.

But hey, that's Al, white shirt and a bow tie, even at a picnic. They arrive at their building, Ricky pays the cab driver, and they all go into the lobby to call for the elevator and go up to their respective floors. They thank each other for sharing a wonderful evening together. Al and Alice thanked them again for looking after their plants while they are out of town, and then they said goodnight. Ricky and Sara go up to their apartment. Once inside, Ricky removes Sara's wrap and as he does, he just stops in his tracks, just to look at her. Her beautiful, long, dark, red hair was flowing over that fitted, forest green cocktail dress. This is what she had worn to the restaurant but Ricky only seemed to notice, really notice now.

Sara turns gently toward him and smiles. "Sir, you are truly a genius and the luckiest man I know. Now, I want you to sit back and relax. I'm going to get two brandy snifters and pour us some Courvoisier."

Ricky looks up at her. "And then?"

She looks at him, smiles, and leans into him, she whispers, "After we finish the brandy, I need you to take me to bed, is that okay?"

He pulls back a bit, and looks deeply into her sparkling green, cat-like eyes, and replies softly, "Pour the brandy."

They sip the brandy and talk about the events that have occurred. How finally everything seems to be falling into place. First, an opportunity presents itself allowing Ricky to arrange a data package hand-off with John Klegman. He will achieve this by appraising and surveying the adjacent site. Then he needs to conceive a way to implicate Al and Alice using some kind of made-up scheme as a surveillance decoy. That can only happen with access to their apartment. Now he will have that access on Wednesday and he will be able to carry out the next and most critical phase of the plan, the data capture, and manipulation of his device. They finish their conversation and their brandies and then Sara takes Ricky by the hand and leads him to the bedroom. As they enter the bedroom, she lets her dress slide off, down to the floor, and then…the lights go…*out.*

The next day, Tuesday, Ricky and Sara go about their morning routine and resume their regular work schedule. He contacts the government officials from his home office phone to get the scheduled dates for a walk-through of the land sites to see if they are suitable for their needs. When they receive the land survey data from Ricky, they will then decide whether to acquire one or more of the pieces of land contained in the proposal. The representative that takes the call puts Ricky on hold while he looks up possible dates for a walk-through. Ricky needs to observe the pieces of land to determine the crew, the equipment, and the necessary time needed to be able to do his job. He also knows that walking the site next to John's building he can scout an area of the site that would work for the data package hand-off.

The rep comes back on the phone with the site, and available date information, "Hello, Ricky, there is only one site to be seen as soon as possible, it is the one located at 1201 Broadview Ave near the department of defense facility. There are two dates available at this time; it can be either this, Friday, or next Wednesday. The onsite meet time is ten am. So, which date do you want?"

Ricky asks for a moment to check his calendar and the rep agrees. He does not know if the package is ready now or not. He has not heard from John. The rep was still waiting for an answer.

Finally, Ricky says, "Okay, okay, next Wednesday will be best."

The rep confirms the date and time with Ricky, he puts it on the calendar and it was set. Ricky gets up and goes into the bedroom. He keeps his special phone in a lockbox. He powers up the phone and after it loads, he checks for email or messages from John, nothing. With no word from John, Ricky grabs his Yankees blue satin team jacket, goes downstairs, and exits the building. He hails a cab and tells the driver, "1201 Broadview Ave."

He wants to go check the site area and to see how the property entrance is secured. He arrives, exits the cab, turns, and finds himself face-to-face with a seven-foot-high chain-link fence. Something on the fence obscured his vision of the property. Upon closer inspection, he sees a very fine meshing weaved throughout the surface area of each fence section. Ricky walks up to the only entrance, the main gate. The gate is locked with a heavy chain draped around the gate and the gatepost. It is locked together with a heavy-duty, keyed padlock. Ricky takes note of the lock brand and its physical size. Then he takes a picture of the lock with his phone camera He hails a cab and while he is waiting, he looks up hardware stores in New York City. Looking for the nearest one that would have what he needs. He finds a lock specialist hardware store on 3rd Ave. Only a few miles away heading back downtown. When a cab finally stops to pick him up, he has the driver bring him to the hardware store. He arrives at the store, pays the cab, and goes inside. Once inside, a store assistant asks Ricky if can help him. "Hello sir, my name is Ralph, do you need any assistance?"

"Hello Ralph, I'm Ricky, pleasure to meet you. Can you tell me where I might find the Branston padlocks?"

"Yes sir, aisle number eight, about half-way down the aisle on your, uh, on your left."

"That's great Ralph, thank you."

"You're welcome, sir."

Ricky heads through the store and into aisle number eight. He views all the various locks on display. Some of them looked the same. He takes out his phone to view the picture of the lock on the gate. He enlarges the images on the screen looking for valid identifiable markings. After slowly scanning the photo, he spots a small engraving, and he enlarges it further. Then he sees, BRN45HV. He scans the display of locks looking to find the lock that bears that number. After several minutes of looking, he finds the right lock. It's a match, and now he has the keys. He just needs to figure out a way to swap the locks. Ricky pays for the lock in cash, leaves, and hails a cab to go home. As he is sitting in the cab, he checks his phone, still no word from John. When he gets home, he tries John again, no response. He goes into the bedroom and puts the lock in his top dresser drawer. He will not need it until Wednesday. He walks out of the bedroom, into the living room, and starts pacing back and forth, as his mind is overloading a bit. *Where is John?* he thought. *It is not like him. I have to call him; I have to know where we are with the package.*

Ricky hesitates for a moment then dials the number again to reach John's special phone. It is ringing, no one is answering yet. It rings a couple more times then, nothing. It was as if someone pressed a button to end the call. He begins to think, *that should not have happened. Because of the code required to gain access to the phone, the only one that can use that phone or make a call from John's phone is John. Besides the code, there is fingerprint and retina scan security.* Now, he was concerned, *he should have been able to leave an encoded message for John.* He sits down in a blue-grey leather recliner in the living room and starts thinking about the fact he needs to report to captain Yurjinsky soon and he cannot go back without good news. *I am sure that John has just been busy, data analysts in his position usually are. I will try him again later.* He now focuses on the time frame he had been given to complete this task; he remembers the captain's words *the clock is ticking.* The site walk-through next Wednesday is the only time he will have to pick out and set the drop zone. He will then notify John with the exact coordinates for the drop. The package must be ready then, period. There is no margin for error. He will return to the site after nightfall Wednesday evening and retrieve the package. It is not government property yet but it is city-owned and tied up in a legal dispute. He will need to think of a way to be in and out. He will have the package in time for his meeting with the captain. With this as his mindset, he leans back in the recliner, closes his eyes, and he falls asleep. A short time later, he woke up. He gets up from the recliner, rubbing his eyes, and goes into the kitchen, to make a cup of coffee.

Sitting at the table he calls out, "play jazz," and like before the music began to play. He remembers this was what gave him the idea of how to implicate the neighbors. Tomorrow, he will have a key to walk into their apartment and perform his hi-tech magic.

He sits and smiles, and he thinks. *I cannot believe how all of this is just falling into place. I will have the key to their apartment, I will be able to capture their I.D. information, and then I will be able to complete the project at home.*

From that moment on, when Sara and I put this plan into effect, we will be free to move around, free of suspicion because they will be watching...

He sits up. "Oh, no," he yells out! "They will be watching no one! Al and Alice are not there!"

Ricky just sits there staring into space, he becomes white with fear, and glistening beads of sweat break out across his forehead and run down the sides of his face. He then begins to mumble to himself, quietly, *what am I going to do, what am I going to do? If I can't redirect their attention away from me, how will I be able to make the pick-up?*

Seemingly, on the edge of a mini breakdown, he just as suddenly snaps out of it. A strange calm comes over him. He now looks as if the shock has passed as the color returns to his face. He sits down at the kitchen table and thinks about it for a moment, *I will talk it over tonight with Sara. We will figure something out.* Sara arrives home from work around seven p.m. She tells him about what a harrowing day she had, running to the office, running to court. Then after court, she had to go back to the office and update the computer before she was done for the day.

"So, how was your day, Ricky?"

"Well, I had quite a day myself. It started with me getting a date for a site walk-through."

"Is it the one near John's work?"

"Yes; that was the only site they want seen as soon as possible."

"That's great, when is it going to happen?"

"It will be next Wednesday, at ten am. I have not heard from John in days and he did not answer my call. I need a status on the package."

"You'll get it, John is very good at what he does, don't worry, you'll get it."

"Yes, I'm sure you're right, John is the best. There was just one more wrinkle I came across today."

"A wrinkle, what wrinkle?"

"Well, do you remember my brilliant plan to try and implicate the neighbors?"

"Yes, it's a great idea."

"Thank you, though right now there is a missing component."

"Really, what would that be?"

"Well, in order to cast suspicion on someone, they have to be present, wouldn't you agree?"

Sara froze and the smile left her face. She looks at him. "What are we going to do? We can't do anything with them watching us."

"I know, Sara, but I don't know what to do about it yet."

"We need to think of something fast."

He looks at her with a strong look of confidence in his eyes.

"Sara, we have one week, we'll think of something. Al said they would only be gone three to maybe five days. Three days is Friday. Five days means they will be back no later than Sunday. I'm going to stay with the plan. I will capture the data from their device and modify our device. Now we need to begin the implication even before they return. We need to create the scenario now."

"What can I do to help?"

He's silent for a second or two. "You know, Sara, you can help me out on this. Do you remember the mission assignment when we had to acquire the Satellite Transmission codes?"

"Yes, I remember."

"Well, what if we use that scenario except we make it submarine launch codes instead?"

She thinks about the idea for a moment. "How do you want to go about it?"

"We will create a simple dialog; we will discuss a meeting place and time. Let's go into the bedroom to discuss this."

Inside the bedroom, he speaks softly in Russian to her, "Are we set for the meeting at the pier? Did you confirm the time and day?"

"Then you would respond: 'Yes, I confirmed with headquarters, next Wednesday at seven p.m., Basil Cunyev will meet us.'

"Then me: 'Will he have the codes?'

"You: 'Yes.'

"Me: 'Did he confirm the pier number with you?'

"You: 'Yes he did, Pier 17.'

"Me: 'That's good news, very good news. Once we have the codes, we can be on the next plane home.'

"That's it, Sara, that's the script, it works."

"Yes, and that will take them all downtown while we take care of business uptown."

"Sara, we need to rehearse this script so it flows, naturally."

"Yes, that's fine with me, Ricky. I think this is going to work."

"I agree, let's go down to the mailbox in the morning and get the key. Then we will go up to their apartment, you can tend to the plants and I will tend to the device."

Wednesday morning, they leave the apartment and take the elevator down the lobby. They first go out to a deli to get their morning coffee. When they return, they walk across the lobby to the mailroom. Ricky opens the mailbox and the key is there. He takes the key, closes the mailbox and they take the elevator up to the tenth floor. When they exit the elevator, Ricky's cell phone receives a notification. He takes out his phone and he sees himself and Sara on the screen.

He turns to Sara, "I forgot to take down the camera, wait here."

He runs down the hallway toward the stairwell and the fire extinguisher where he had previously set up one of his surveillance cameras. He reaches up behind the unit and takes the camera down then he shuts it down. He walks back up the hall to Sara and they enter Al and Alice's apartment. Sara immediately sets about taking care of the plants and flowers as she had agreed. Ricky uses his special phone to help him locate their device quickly. He finds it in their den and goes about his task to obtain the data he needs to make the switch. Sara completes her task and shortly thereafter Ricky completes his.

They leave the apartment, lock the door, and go back up to their apartment. When they get back upstairs, Sara gathers her things and heads to her office. Ricky starts to work on the project carefully laying out the schematic strategy to modify his own listening device. He works out the details for the project all day. Sara comes home around five-thirty.

"Hello, I'm home," she calls out.

"I'm in the living room, Sara."

"Hi, any luck?"

"Yes, the schematic is almost done."

"Why don't we get some dinner, I will complete it when we return."

"Sounds good, I missed lunch, are you ready to go?"

"Yes, let's go."

They go out for dinner to a favorite small, local, Italian restaurant, Giorgio's. He explains to Sara what he had done so far and what is still to be done. They return from dinner, and he returns to the device schematic to complete the changes necessary to accomplish his plan.

"Ricky, it's getting late, I have another early, busy day, I'm exhausted and I am going to bed."

"Okay, I will be done shortly and then I will join you, goodnight."

Thursday morning Ricky calls his office and he has his admin move his morning appointments to later in the afternoon or tomorrow. He needs time now to make the components that are required for the modifications to his device. Once this is done, they will be ready to deliver their script and shift the eyes of the watchers to Al and Alice. Sara had gone into the office while Ricky stayed at home to work on and complete the project. He shuts down the unit and opens it. He can manipulate the device and cancel the output signal of the device using a small connector known as a 'jumper.' With this jumper in the right place when the device is activated it will only emit an internal signal. No external broadcast will be sent.

He installs the modifications and when he was done, he needs to give it a test. He powers the unit up, it's working. His special cell phone can detect this internal signal so through his phone he can hear what they will hear.

He speaks aloud, "Hello, play jazz."

He hears his command through the phone but no jazz played because there was no external broadcast.

"Okay," he said aloud. Next, he speaks in Russian and scans his phone's screen to see which device I.D. appears his or theirs? He hears his voice audio through his phone and noted the I.D. transmitted; it was Al's. Then just to be sure that the switch was working correctly, he did another test in English. His I.D. came up, and it works perfectly. He shuts the device down and removes the jumper in order to restore the unit's external broadcast capabilities. He takes his time to reassemble the unit. He turns it on and it is ready to go. He did it, he was able to make the device respond and transmit a different I.D. code based on the language spoken.

He sends a text to Sara, 'I'm done, going to the office for a couple of meetings, see you later.' He leaves the building and he hails a cab to take him to his office. He gets to his office and tends to his appointments. He finishes with both clients and then he heads home. That evening, he and Sara went into the bedroom and shut the door. They needed to rehearse their script away from any surveillance. After a while they had it down, they were ready. Ricky wants to check the current surveillance positions outside. This way, after they broadcast the script, he will be able to tell when their focus shifts away from them. He goes into the bedroom, goes into the closet and he takes out a black leather case. Inside there are several very thin body, wide-angle, HD cameras. Some with a night vision option and a non-reflective screen. When needed, the camera can be mounted on a sleek 18-inch gooseneck. This flexible extension plugs directly into his phone. He stands near the front window, just off to the side. He slowly slides the wafer-thin camera behind the curtain, lens facing the window. He turns on his phone to view the scene outside and he sees the watchers. He zooms in to take note of the direction of their surveillance equipment. The rooftop cameras on the van across the street, the large, coned microphones they use to pick up audio.

All of their equipment certainly seems to be focused on the 11th floor. He withdraws the camera. He has enough footage to compare positions after the broadcast.

He turns to Sara, "Listen, we need to wait."

"Wait, wait for what?"

"We need to wait for them to return home."

"Why?"

"This building is being watched."

"Yes, I know."

"No, I mean they watch the patterns of who goes in and out and when just like I did with Al and Alice. It is standard surveillance 101. You study the familiar patterns in order to be able to spot an anomaly. They will know they have not seen Al and Alice for a few days and that is a break in the pattern so they watch harder. This is why we need them to return before we broadcast. The watchers will take notice of their return; they will continue to watch closely. After a day or so they will see the original pattern restored and the intense observation will slacken."

She looks at him. "Okay Ricky, I understand, you're right, we do have to wait. Tomorrow is Friday they could be back tomorrow."

"Yes, tomorrow I will try again to get in touch with John, I still have not heard from him."

"You could go and see the captain. If something happened to John, he would know."

"Don't say that, Sara!"

"What did I say?"

"If something has happened to John, there is no other inside man, no package. Wait, be quiet, my phone just went off."

"What do you mean?"

"We must have said something, maybe a keyword that activated the device."

"It is listening to us right now. Speak softly, let's go inside the bedroom, and quietly close the door."

Once inside, they were out of the audio reception range of the device. They were able to continue the conversation about John for a while.

"Listen, one thing we both know is true; nothing travels faster than bad news. So, no news is good news. Let's get some sleep Sara, I will call John tomorrow."

Friday morning Sara is up and off to work and Ricky makes some phone calls to some associates to inquire casually about John to see what he can find out instead of just constantly failing to reach him. He doesn't gather any specific data but one of them mentioned that he had spoken with John a day or so ago on another matter. Ricky felt a little better, at least John is okay and he's still there. He calls John's phone right away, still no answer but at least now, he can leave an encoded message. He simply asked John to call back at any time. It was now around one in the afternoon; the neighbors have not yet returned. Ricky went to his office to take care of some business deals he had to finish and submit to underwriting for processing. There is nothing more to do now except wait. Wait to hear from John, wait for the neighbors to return, wait for this mission to conclude successfully. Turn the package over to the captain and then collect the big payoff. Later that evening, while they are having dinner, Ricky's special phone rings. He gets up and goes into the bedroom to get the phone, it was John. "Hello, John, are you alright?"

"Hey, Ricky, yes I'm fine man, we have been going 24-7 on some emergency project, and it's been maddening. There is no time to sleep, just analyze freaking data!"

"Is that still going on?"

"Yes, but now my team gets a week off."

"A week off, that's great. Sounds like just what you need after a week like that, John. By the way, where are we? I mean, what is the status of the package?"

"I have should have it all done by Monday, Tuesday the latest."

"I will have a little more time now to put it all together and finish it up."

"Okay John, Monday would be perfect but Tuesday still works."

"Ricky, did you figure out a way for me to hand-off the package to you?"

"Yes, Okay, here it is, but wait, first tell me where you are standing right now."

"Well, I am about 50 or 60 yards due east of the barracks, by the back-fence line, near the wooded area behind the property, why?"

"Next Wednesday, I am going to be on the property next to your facility."

"Why are you going to be there and how are you getting in?"

"It's a proposed land acquisition visit. As a formality, I will be there with some government officials. I will be walking the grounds and surveying the site. I will look for the wooded area on the opposite side of the fence approximately where you are standing right now."

"I am listening, Ricky, go on."

"I will use my phone to take images of the wooded area. I will send the images and their exact survey coordinates to your phone. You will then use your phone to locate the coordinates and thus the area of the drop zone. All you need to do is walk out to the spot where you are now and toss the package over the fence as near to the landing spot as possible, that's it."

"That's it?"

"Well, yes, except this one thing, what time will the package be in the drop zone?"

"Probably like now, right around eight p.m. Is that good for you?"

"Yes, I will be there to pick it up after dark like eight-thirty. I will get the package and go. Are you good with this, John?"

"Yes, listen, Ricky, I have to go, we will talk and you will have your package."

Ricky felt a little uneasy after the call. He thought talking with John and going over the plan would have put him at ease but it didn't. Something just didn't feel right. Ricky went back to the kitchen table to finish dinner and talk with Sara about the call.

"Was that John?"

"Yes."

"Is everything alright?"

"I'm not sure."

"Not sure?"

"I don't know Sara, it's probably just me. John said the reason he had not been in touch was because he was working around the clock on an emergency."

"You don't believe him?"

"I didn't say that, but there was just something, sorry I can't explain it any better than that."

"Did you go over the plan to obtain the package?"

"Yes, John said the package would be completed Monday, Tuesday at the latest."

"Okay, then we're all set."

"Yes, it's all set. I will send the drop zone coordinates to John after I walk the site Wednesday morning. The package will be in the drop zone by eight o'clock Wednesday evening."

"And then?"

"Then, I will hail a cab to bring me to the site. I will pay him and tell him not to wait. I will then go to the drop zone and find the package. I will go back out to the street, walk few blocks to make sure the surrounding area is all clear, then hail another cab and return here, with the package."

Sara looks at him, smiles, and says, "Alright, we're almost home."

They relax a bit after dinner with a couple of brandies and some classical music, Mozart was a favorite as was Ravel's *'Bolero.'* After a while of listening and drinking, they turn everything off and go to bed.

They awaken to a beautiful Saturday morning. Ricky gets up, gets dressed, and goes out to bring home breakfast. Sara stays in bed a little while longer. When he returns, he sets breakfast out on the table and he lets her know that he is back. She comes out of the bedroom looking like she could have maybe slept a little longer. She goes into the kitchen and finds Ricky there, eating his breakfast and smiling like the proverbial 'cat that ate the canary.'

She looks at him curiously and asks, "So, what's up?"

He sets his breakfast down on the table and takes a sip of his coffee.

Chapter 5

He looks up at her. "Guess who came home today?"

She smiles. "The neighbors?"

"Yes, they are home. We need to give them a little time to get settled, then we will go downstairs, knock on the door, say hello and give them back their key."

"When will we do the broadcast?"

He thinks about it for a moment before he responds. "It's Saturday, they need to be seen by the watchers at least a few times in order to lessen the surveillance, remember?"

"Yes, that's what you had said."

"We need to rehearse the script again a few times prior to the broadcast anyway. We will do it Monday evening just before they leave for dinner, around six o'clock. The watchers will hear the script audio in Russian. When they scan the broadcast, Al and Alice's I.D. will come up. They will certainly trace this I.D. for ownership credentials. That information will lead them straight to Al and Alice. When they go out for dinner on Monday night, *they* will be the ones being watched."

About an hour or so later Ricky tells Sara, "Let's go downstairs now."

They go down to visit Al and Alice to finish up that part of the plan. They were invited in and Al and Alice were grateful that they took such great care of all their plants.

"You guys did a wonderful job," Alice told them. "The plants appear to be thriving."

"Our pleasure," said Sara.

Ricky walks over to Al and hands him back the apartment key. "Here you go Al. Here's your key."

Al smiles and shakes Ricky's hand. "Thank you, Ricky, you too, Sara, thank you both very much."

Sara asks, "So how was your trip, Alice?"

"Oh, it was just great, Sara. We got to go home and see our family and friends. That's always great. Not to mention how great it is getting out of this crazy city for a little while, just great."

"Well, it sounds like you had a real good time and a nice break from everyday life, and you, Al?"

"Yeah, I did, Sara, always great to go back home and it's always great to come back home after your trip."

Ricky turns to Sara, "Ready to go, Sara?"

"Sure."

As Sara and Ricky turn to leave, they say, "Have a good day and welcome home."

They go back upstairs to relax.

Once back in their apartment Sara asks Ricky, "Hey, tomorrow is Sunday, do you think we can lay low for one day?"

He looks at her and smiles. "Sure, tomorrow we will lay back. It will all begin on Monday."

Sunday morning, they sleep in. Ricky gets up around eleven-thirty; he calls the local deli and orders breakfast for two to be delivered. He also has them bring a Sunday newspaper. He puts on a pot of coffee and waits for breakfast to be delivered. As breakfast arrives, Sara awakens.

Ricky sees her getting out of bed and says, "No, no, we're going to have breakfast in bed and read the paper."

Sara smiles, turns around, and goes right back to bed. Ricky brings the food and coffee into the bedroom and they enjoy a break in the routine. Sara winks at him. "Did this come with dessert?"

He smiles. "I'll check out the box and let you know."

They emerge from the bedroom around four p.m., Ricky's special phone sounds; it's John.

Ricky answers, "Hello?"

"Ricky, it is John."

"Yes, I know it's you, do you have an update for me?"

"Yes, the package is complete."

"It's ready now, John?"

"Yes, listen; let me describe the package to you I do not have much time. It is a small, grey, corrugated box, about five inches square and an inch and half thick. It is fully padded, with a waterproof wrapping inside and out. Then I sealed the package with a very special infrared tape. You can use the infrared light on your phone to locate it. Well, what do you think, Ricky?"

"That sounds good, just one minute. Alright John, I've got it. Good work getting this done, I'm sure you will receive high praise from our superior for your efforts. I will stay with the plan and the timing we discussed previously. You remember the plan right, right, John?"

"Yes, sure, Wednesday evening at eight o'clock, I remember."

"Okay good, thanks John. We're almost home."

The call ends and Ricky feels better this time as John appeared to be more like John. Maybe he was burnt out like he said. He tells Sara about the call and then they go into the bedroom, close the door, and begin going over the script making sure they had placed the keywords correctly. This was a critical step because the keywords they use will make the whole thing work. There is a standard list of keyword commands that will activate the device. Words like 'play music' or 'tell me the weather.' Ricky encoded additional keywords for their needs, the dates, times, the item being passed, contact names, these keywords, whether in English or Russian, will trigger the device. He also added keywords that pertain to their mission. Keywords like; lasers, weapons, gun, guns, laser data, armed men, the package, murder, murderer, and captain.

If they incorporate any of these keywords into a conversation, it will trigger the device and produce a different result with the watchers and who they alert for each keyword used. After their review of the modified script, they began rehearsing their parts. When they were finished rehearsing it was time for dinner. They decide to go out for dinner. They leave the building, take a short walk up Riverside Drive, and go into Riverside Park to go to the Boat Basin Café.

When they return home, Ricky's special phone was beeping; there's a message from John. He listens to the message, "Ricky, it is John. The rest of my week off has been revoked. I have to report tomorrow morning. I'm sorry but I cannot keep our plan. The package is ready now so I am going to throw it over the fence tonight. Go and pick it up tonight, sorry."

Ricky knows he can't do that. He calls John back.

"Hello," John answered like he was sleeping.

"John, wake up, it's Ricky."

"Yes, Ricky, did you get my message?"

"Yes, I did and that is unacceptable."

"What do you mean?"

"I mean we stick to the plan; I cannot possibly go tonight. The gate is locked, and I am being watched. I am going to do as I planned on Wednesday. I don't care what you have to do to get it done, just get it done. There is too much at stake. I will send the coordinates Wednesday and you will deliver the package to the specified drop zone. Do as I say, John, no changes. Wednesday as planned. Do you copy, John?"

"Yes Ricky, yes, I copy. Somehow, I will do it, send me the data when you have it, goodnight."

Ricky puts the phone down and he was annoyed and confused at what exactly is taking place. He goes into the living room and tells Sara of the exchange. "Something is going on, what do you know about it?"

"Me, I know what you know."

"What do you know about John?"

"John, what do you mean, what about him?"

"His erratic behavior lately, I mean no contact then a kind of strange contact followed by normal contact. Then the message he left on my phone that the drop had to be tonight. Yet when I called him back and scratched that, he said he'll do it on Wednesday. I don't understand all of the back and forth, why is he acting like this, do you have any ideas?"

"Ricky, will you please stop pacing, and sit down."

He sits down on the sofa and takes a breath. "So, any thoughts about John," he asks again.

"Well, I do agree his behavior patterns are a little off, maybe he is truly getting burnt out."

"You know his job is very intense and he can never leave the premises. Maybe after this much time inside for him, it begins to feel like he is in prison. You know, maybe he gets a little stir crazy."

"Maybe you're right, Sara. He has been working inside for years. I know it would certainly get to me after a while."

"You know that the only vacation he gets is when he is asleep."

"Yes, yes, I understand that Sara. It's a difficult lifestyle. I have also learned that the captain has him working on a few jobs not just ours."

"How do you know that?"

"He smiles. "Didn't you say earlier, 'I know what you know,' and he laughs."

She looks at him and demands, "Tell me how you know that!"

"Okay, okay, take it easy. The other day I reached out to a few associates. I was attempting to see if anyone else had contact with John. One of them said he had spoken with John on his own business topic a few days ago. So that means John is running at least two schemes at the same time."

"It's probably why he's been acting so strange."

"I'm not sure, Sara. It's getting late, what do you say, do you want to call it a night?"

"Fine with me, I have to be in court at nine am."

"Tomorrow is Monday Sara. We will put our plan into effect tomorrow evening."

They disappear into the bedroom and shut the door.

Chapter 6

Monday morning starts a new work week. They get up, go about their business and leave for work. Sara returns from work around five p.m. Ricky arrives at five forty-five p.m. When he goes into the building, he asks Charles the doorman if Al and Alice had come home. Charles Beekman is in his early 30s; he has dark brown hair and eyes. He is powerfully built and stands over six feet tall.

"Yes Mr. Rogers, they came in a short time ago, sir."

"Thank you Charles. Have a good evening."

Ricky walks to the elevator and goes up to the apartment.

He finds Sara and tells her, "It's almost six o'clock, are you ready?"

"Yes, I am ready."

He goes into the bedroom and gets the scripts. He hands her a copy. He quickly goes back to the bedroom to get another small surveillance camera.

"I want to take a look at their surveillance tonight before we broadcast."

He quickly grabs the setup of the camera and gooseneck and connects it to his phone. Then he slides the camera gently behind the curtains as he had done previously. He activates the camera from the phone app and the view is the same as the other night.

"Okay, they are all set in the same position as always, let's do the broadcast."

He begins immediately to perform the script dialog with Sara. It goes smoothly. When they are done, he grabs his camera again to see if they took notice. At first, there seemed to be no change. He pulls the camera back and looks at Sara.

"Nothing has changed."

"Look again in a few minutes, Ricky. It can take them a little time to trace the I.D. data."

He slides the camera back to the window and he sees no movement. Just as he's about to withdraw the camera he notices the back doors of the van across the street swing open and two agents jump out. They run into the building where the other watchers are also running the remote command center.

He pulls the camera back and turns to Sara, "Something is happening. Two agents just ran into the building across the street."

He waits another few minutes and sets the camera again for another look. "They must have traced the I.D, Sara."

"How can you tell, was there a movement of their equipment?"

"Yes, because now I see all of their surveillance gear is pointing down to the tenth floor."

"It worked, you did it, Ricky."

"We did it, Sara, and we need to do it again tomorrow around the same time."

"We are going to do the same script again, Ricky?"

"No, it will be like a follow-up. Come into the bedroom and close the door. Do you have your copy?"

"Yes, I have it, Ricky."

"Then we will edit the script. Let's go into the bedroom first and shut the door. Let's do it like this. I will ask you, 'Any news from headquarters today?'

"Then you: 'Yes, they made the customary follow-up call to again go over the details.'

"Then me: 'Were there any changes?'

"Then you: 'Yes, we are now meeting with Paul Krinsky, not Basil Cunyev.'

"Then me: 'Is that all?'

"Then you: 'Yes, the meet is still Wednesday at seven p.m., Pier 17.'

"Stop, that's it, that was great, Sara. That is the script we will use tomorrow night."

He looks at his watch. "It's almost seven p.m.; I am going to aim the camera to view down toward the front of the building and down to the street."

"Why are you doing that?"

"This way I will be able to see Al and Alice leave the building for dinner and see who and how many follow them."

"Alright, Ricky, do you want to order dinner in?"

"Sure, are you thinking what I'm thinking?"

"Let me guess, Ricky, Giorgio's?"

"Yes."

"Do you want the usual, veal ala Giorgio's?"

"Yes, that sounds great."

"Okay, I am going to call to place our order."

"Sara, wait a second!"

"Wait, wait to place the order?"

"No, no order, Al and Alice are leaving the building now. I want to see what happens."

Al and Alice exit the building, and they go right heading west. After about a minute, the van doors open, four agents exit the van. Two of them appear to be armed. They slowly walk across the street and start heading west. Sara finishes placing the order for their dinner. Ricky turns and tells her, "Four agents started to follow them, two appear to be armed. After dinner tonight, Sara, we will take a walk to go out for a cappuccino. I need to find out if anyone even bothers to follow us now."

"That's fine with me, Ricky, I love cappuccino."

Dinner arrives around eight. While they have dinner, they review the plans and the new script. When they finish dinner, they go out as planned. They go out of the building and start off to the right heading west.

When they get to the end of 79th Street at Riverside Drive, they stop, turn around and walk back heading east on 79th.

"Sara, if the watchers are looking for us, that about-face should trigger a reaction."

They continue to walk east on 79th Street. They have to stop at one point about three minutes into the walk so Sara can adjust her shoe straps. While she does this, Ricky takes out his phone, opens the camera app, and sets it to the night-vision mode. Looking at the view on the screen, he scans the area behind them down the street to try and detect any movement. No images appear on the screen. With the night-vision engaged, his screen displays a near daylight view of the street.

He tells Sara, "It looks like we're not being followed."

She finishes adjusting the strap on her shoe and they continue on to the coffee shop. They get their cappuccinos to go and drink them slowly as they walk back to the building. All was quiet in the area when they arrived. They go in, go upstairs, and relax for a while before going to bed.

Ricky tells Sara, "We will need to review the revised script to make sure that we did not eliminate any of the keywords. We should also rehearse it again."

"We don't need to rehearse it again, Ricky, it's good as it is."

"No Sara, we need to do it at least one more time before the next broadcast."

"All right, tomorrow evening let's both be here by five-thirty and we will do it then. I'm tired now Ricky, and we both have work in the morning; I am going to bed, goodnight."

He kisses her goodnight. "I will be there in a minute I am going to check the street again."

Now that they had come home, he wanted to scan the surveillance for any changes. He sets up the camera and sees that the view is the same. All of the equipment is still focused on one floor below. He withdraws the camera and goes to bed. Tuesday morning they get up and go to work. Sara left the office early and went downtown.

She had arranged a meeting over the phone with another interested party that said they will pay her well for the package. They meet at a small Italian bistro in the Little Italy section of lower Manhattan. They had cocktails and talked for a while. They couldn't reach a deal so they left. As they were leaving, they said they would be in touch.

After they left the meeting, Sara looked at her watch and saw it was almost four-thirty. She takes out her phone and calls a car service to bring her home. Before Ricky leaves for his day, he realizes that he needs a way to get Al and Alice to go to the pier on Wednesday. He enters the lobby and sees a stack of flyers on the lobby desk, a flyer stating there is a street fair event at Chelsea Pier boasting great food and free entertainment. He remembers Al saying at the piano bar how they love going to Chelsea Pier. He takes a flyer and goes to his office. When he returns Tuesday evening, before he goes upstairs, he goes over to apartment mailboxes. He finds their mailbox, folds the flyer, and slides it into the slot but not completely so it will be visible. The Chelsea Pier is very close to where both Al and Alice work. This is how I will have them show up at the pier. The watchers will be set up well in advance based on what they had heard in the broadcast. The fact that Al and Alice were to meet at seven and then show up early means nothing. The watchers will simply think that seven p.m. time in the broadcast was a decoy time. Al and Alice will see the flyer sticking out of their mailbox in the morning. Wednesday night after work they will meet and go to the pier. When Al and Alice arrive at the pier the watchers will notice and begin to follow them. They will watch but they will not see them meet or speak with anyone as far as they can tell. They know they can't make a move prematurely so they will just continue to watch. In any case, if Al and Alice are a 'no-show,' the watchers will mark the disclosed secret meeting event as a decoy and eventually leave the Pier. Ricky and Sara meet back at the apartment around five-thirty. They order dinner in, go into the bedroom and close the door.

They review the new script for any missing keywords as a result of the edit of the original script. The keywords were all still in place. Dinner arrives and after dinner, they run through the script one time, it's now almost seven o'clock. They go into the living room and perform the follow-up broadcast. When they were done, he again sets up his camera to look and see if there is a response. This time the van doors opened and two agents exited the van almost immediately after the follow-up broadcast.

He turns to Sara, "They reacted very quickly this time."

"Sure they did, this time they did not have to trace the I.D."

"Alright Sara, tomorrow is Wednesday; tomorrow we will be able to finish."

"Finish, we still need to get the package to the captain, did you forget that?"

He looks at her and says, "No Sara, I did not forget that. I was only referring to finally being able to acquire the package. That is what will be finished. Why would you think I would forget reporting to the captain? Why would you even say that?"

She just looks at him and stands there in hushed silence. He goes to power down the device and begins restoring it to normal function. He was finishing up and then... "Listen, Ricky, it would not be the first time you sold out your superior to the authorities. You give them up anonymously and then sell the stolen information to the highest private bidder for cash."

"Who told you that?"

"John."

"John Klegman?"

"John told you that, what else did he tell you?"

"He told me that on one of the jobs he let you know about a private investor. He said that the investor wanted the same data, and was willing to pay cash, in the millions."

"John Klegman told you this?"

"Yes, then he said you and he had an agreement to split the money evenly, and you didn't honor that agreement."

"Okay, well it sounds like he told you everything."

"No, there's more, John also told me that in order to pull off a cash deal; the superior for the job has to be given up. You know, an unnamed informant tips off the feds about a bunch of men in a basement apartment. They are speaking in a foreign language and they all have weapons."

"That all sounds pretty fantastic, and I did all this?"

"Yes, that is what John told me, is it true?"

"Sara, no, I have never made a private deal arrangement with anyone. In this business, you know as well as I, there is always a rat. If I had done as you say, I would not be here now. Someone would have talked and I would be dead. I think John was telling you a tale, a dream perhaps. When did you have this conversation with John?"

She hesitates for a moment. "I guess it was about three weeks ago."

"Three weeks ago, so why did you wait to confront me, why bring it up now?"

"I don't know, I guess if it was true and you were working a deal on this job, I wanted to be in on it."

He looks at her sternly. "No deals, I just want this piece of the mission to be done. I will feel better when I have the package and yes, I am bringing it to the captain, no sellout.

It's getting late, we have a big day tomorrow, let's go to bed."

"Well, I only brought it up because if that is what's going down on this job I want to know, and I want my cut."

"Nothing is going down but the plan, period. No sellouts, no phony phone calls, and no cash deals. We need to report after we complete the exchange. We wrap this up Wednesday night and we will go see the captain Thursday. Sara, have you ever worked with Captain Yurjinsky before?"

"No."

"Well neither have I, the word on the street is he's crazy. They say that when you present him the completed job, he examines it. As long as the job was done correctly, you are given an attaché case filled with money, around two million dollars. Otherwise, you are paid for your services in a much harsher fashion. Now let's get some sleep."

Wednesday morning, they get up for work around eight a.m. Sara was going to court again this morning and Ricky was on his way to view the site.

While in the cab he calls John, "Hello?"

"John, it's Ricky."

"Yes Ricky, do you have the data already?"

"No not yet."

"What is it then?"

"Why did you tell Sara, we did a private job?"

"I did not tell her anything."

"She said she spoke with you about three weeks ago."

"Ricky, I have not spoken with your Sara, ever."

"Then where did she come up with this story, and why?"

"I don't know, Ricky; you better watch your back. It sounds like you're being played. You are still sending the data, right?"

"Yes, I'm almost on site now, out."

He arrives at the property site address, 1201 Broadview Ave. at nine forty-five and he is the first one there. He examines the padlock used on the chain locking the gate. It is the same one he had seen previously. He puts his survey gear bag on his shoulder and walks up the street to a deli for a cup of coffee. He has the new lock in his dark green canvas equipment bag. When he returns to the site, he sees the government officials are there.

They meet and talk for a few minutes then Ricky takes his surveying gear and they begin to walk the property. The officials walk several paces behind him continuing their conversations. Ricky stops to set up his equipment for the first part of the survey.

He tells the officials, "I am going to need multiple views from various locations throughout the property, this is just the first."

They look at him and nod in approval. Then they resume their conversations talking amongst themselves, paying little attention to him. He completes the survey from the first position and continues to move around the site collecting his data. As he continues to make his way around the grounds, he passes a line of tall, thick, evergreen trees. They range in height between eight to ten feet. At the end of the line of trees, he comes to a section that bends around to the right. This is when Ricky first sees the wooded area near the fence line. John had described it to him on the call. He needs to get near that wooded area in order to be able to get the drop zone data. He begins walking in that direction.

He is about halfway to the spot when the officials start yelling, "Hey!"

"What are you doing?"

They start moving toward him waving their arms. "Not that section, just along this fence line."

"You are not allowed back there."

He thinks for a moment before he responds. "I know this is not part of the property for the survey. I need to be here to get my readings over there. He points toward the western perimeter of the site. It will only take a few minutes. Without it, I won't be able to submit the required specifications. Please, let me do my job, I will be done soon."

The officials move up a little closer, still watching him but not too closely. He can now get close enough to the wooded area to get the data. At one point he flips his survey gear around and takes readings of the wooded area. Then he takes out his phone and takes a few quick images of the area. He quickly turns his gear around, begins break it down, and pack it up. When packing his gear, he slips the lock out of the bag, and unlocks it. He puts the open lock in his kind of baggy, dark-blue cargo pants pocket so the lock would not be noticeable. He walks over to the officials. "I'm all done gentlemen, thank you for your time."

"I will begin to process the data and forward the results to your office as soon as possible."

They all start to walk off the site together; Ricky is lagging behind a bit. He watches as the officials call for a car to pick them up. As Ricky is nearing the exit, he moves slightly to the right side of the access gate, near the right gate post where the chain and the open lock are hanging. As he passes by the post, he quickly places his new lock on the chain near the original lock and lifts the original from its resting place, and slides it into his pocket. When the security guards come to lock up the gate, they will use his lock. He grabs a cab to take him back to his office to review the site data. He uploads all of the data to his computer. The information is presented in a report format, one report for each section surveyed. When he gets to the wooded area report he takes out his phone and tries to visually match the images to the survey data. Once he has this sorted out, he will have the drop zone. He highlights all the wooded area data, copies it, and saves it to separate document. He then deletes that section of the report removing any of this information. The five-page report is now a four-page report only containing data for the actual property. He saves the site data and closes the file for now. He opens the file with the secret data and starts working on the drop zone. It takes some time but he is able to match the correct images to the survey data. He notes there is a cluster of Pine trees in kind of a horseshoe configuration. From the edge of the clearing just outside the wooded area, the cluster of trees is located twenty-one feet into the woods and six feet in from the back-fence line. He adds each of the images separately with their corresponding survey coordinates to the document, saves the data then sends all of it to his phone. As soon as he receives the file, he forwards it to John's phone. About ten minutes later he receives a notification on his phone from John, confirmed. He goes back to work for a while on the real site file. Around four p.m. he wraps it up and heads for home. During the cab ride, he starts thinking about what is actually going on. *I never did a private job with John. What reason would he have to tell her something like that? Then he said he has never spoken with her, never. If he did not do this, then who did and why? Could it be, it was all Sara? Is she running a private agenda with someone else? I have to find out and soon.* He returns home and Sara is not home yet. Sitting down at the kitchen table, he grabs a note pad and starts to map things out. *First, I need access to her phone log. If they spoke, John's cell number would be there and I will know that John is playing me. If John's number is not there, then it's Sara making up a story. I am so close to the finish line I must know who I can trust.* Just then, the apartment door opens breaking his train of thought, it's Sara.

She sets her briefcase and purse down on a tall glass table in the foyer and calls out, "Hello?"

"I'm in the kitchen, Sara."

He tears out the page with his thoughts and stuffs it in his pocket and he puts the pad back on the counter. "How did the walk-through go?"

"It went well."

"Were you able to get the data you needed?"

"Yes."

"Did you send it to John?"

"Yes."

"Why the one-word answers, is something wrong?"

"Wrong, no why would you think that?"

"I don't know, you just seem a little distant."

"Not at all, I am fine. It was extremely intense doing what I did today. The officials almost stopped me from getting anywhere near the target site."

"Really, what did you do?"

"I worked it out."

Abandoning his earlier plan to try and sneak access to her phones he decides to call her out.

"Oh, I have been meaning to ask you, when you spoke with John was the call placed on your personal phone or your encoded phone?"

She just stares at him. "What do you mean?"

"I believe it was a fairly simple question."

"Why do you need to know?"

"You blurted out some pretty dangerous allegations the other night. You know as well as I that the KGB also listens. You never really know who's listening. You may have issued me a death sentence for something I did not do. Why don't you just answer the question or better still let me see your phones?"

"My phones are mine, period. I'm not giving you my phones. You are calling me a liar."

"You called me a traitor and a thief; liar seems pretty mild. Why won't you just tell me? What are you hiding, Sara?"

"Look, Ricky, I told you, I got a call; he said it was John. Everything I said to you the other night is what he had told me."

"Okay, just get the phone he called you on."

"Why, why do you need to see my phone?"

"Listen to me, Sara, I know I did not participate in any such activity. Therefore, I need to confirm if it was John, or someone claiming to be John. If there is nothing to hide, just get me the phone that you used so I can check the number. If it was not him, then there is a different problem. So please, go and bring me the phone now, please."

Sara walks out of the room, visibly annoyed with Ricky, and goes into the foyer where she had left her briefcase. She opens it and takes out a phone, it was the special phone. He went into the bedroom to get his phone for the number comparison. They meet back in the kitchen and she gives him the phone.

"Here, I already scanned the phone open, check it."

He takes the phone from her and begins scrolling through the logs of inbound and outbound calls.

"I can't find John's number in your phone, not even in contacts. Who called you, Sara?"

"He said it was John, that's all I know."

"Okay, okay Sara, if that's all you know, that's all you know. Thank you for giving me your phone. I have to go get ready to make the pickup."

"Get ready?"

"Yes, I just need to change out of these clothes."

"What about dinner?"

"I'm not really hungry, I had a big lunch. Order something for yourself if you like."

He gets up and goes into the bedroom to change. Sara starts flipping through take out menus. When he had finished changing, he went into the closet in the bedroom and took out another locked case. He opens the case and removes a Glock nine-millimeter handgun, an extra clip, and a silencer. He next pulls out a side-mount shoulder holster, straps it on, slides the gun in, and puts on his dark blue satin Yankee's jacket. He also grabs the original gate lock he had taken that morning. He will replace his lock with the original after he has the package. When he leaves the grounds, he will switch the locks, and then lock the gate with the chain and their lock. He goes into the kitchen and tells her, "I have to go there now to pick up the package."

"Now wait a minute, Ricky, I'm coming with you."

"No Sara, you are not. I am going alone; I don't know what I'm walking into. I have to go."

Ricky leaves, gets a cab, and heads for the site. He arrives and he pays the driver and tells him to go. He immediately takes out the key for the gate lock; he opens it and enters the property. He closes the gate but he does not lock it, the chain is just hanging on the gate. There is little to no lighting on this property. So, not to be seen by passers-by, he uses the infrared scanner on his phone and starts carefully walking the fence line. The infrared scanner will also allow him to spot the package in the wooded area. He rounds the corner of the property and heads toward the wooded area. He wonders if John was able to make the delivery, he did not get a confirmation. It was absolute darkness in the woods now. He literally can't see his hand in front of his face. He begins sweeping the area with his phone, and then, there it is, in the cluster of Pine trees, he finds the package. It was just as John had described it. He picks it up, turns, and starts to make his way out the woods and back to the street to get a cab and go home. He exits the wooded area and moves into the clearing. The area is very dark with only faint traces of light from the distant streetlamps. He turns the corner making his way back out of the property. As he is walking back toward the street, he hears the chain on the gate rattle. Then he notices two large shadowy figures walking on the property coming slowly in his direction. He slows his pace a bit but continues moving forward, still in the deep shadows. At one point as the strangers are approaching, the headlights of a garbage truck, slowly turning the corner, exposes them. They were exposed enough that he could see they were carrying weapons. He stops in the shadows, and slips into the row of tall evergreen trees, that run along the fence line. He quickly affixes the silencer to his gun and then quietly waits. As they continue to advance deeper into the property, they reach the line of evergreen trees. They continue to pass by the evergreens looking for Ricky. Ricky is a bit further up the line and waiting there he hears the unmistakable sound of someone 'racking-the-slide,' of a shotgun. He waits just a few more seconds then, still in deep darkness, he steps out from his cover. He quickly shoots and kills both men. They were Russian Death Squad hitmen, quite possibly sent due to what Sara had said the other night or maybe it was Sara that set this up. Ricky did not want to hang around. He again started making his way to the street. He was approaching the gate when he noticed a car parked at the curb with someone inside. He quickly moves to the right and disappears into the darkness on the west side of the property. He watches as the car door opens and sees what appears to be another Death Squad member. He closes the door of his black Mercedes S-class and approaches the gate. As he very slowly enters the property, the sleeve of his shirt gets snagged on a rough metal barb on the gate. When he pulls free from the gate; a piece of his sleeve tears off and remains there.

Ricky is observing this large individual moving through the property. Then this big man starts to call out in a somewhat hushed voice, "Alex, Reko? It is Dmitri."

No response, he continues to advance deeper into the site and then he trips over something and falls down to the ground. He gets up and when he is brushing himself off, he feels something wet. He takes out his phone and turns on a flashlight app. What he sees turns him cold. His hands are covered in blood. He quickly feels around to see if it was his blood. He finds no evidence of being hurt. Then he turns his phone flashlight toward the ground to see what he had tripped over. His eyes grow large and his facial expression becomes distraught. He sees the two bodies on the ground, and realizes that it was the blood of Alex and Reko. He turns off the flashlight. Standing beside his two slain brothers-in-arms, he bends to retrieve Reko's weapon, a seventeen-round Glock with the silencer attached. He opens fire on the row of evergreens thinking maybe the guy that did this was possibly still hiding there. Dmitri stops and stands silently for a moment to think about the situation. *He did not leave this site through the gate. He is here, I will find him, I will find him and I will kill him.*

He continues to make his way around the property. Every once in a while, he would softly call out, "Ricky, I know you are here, you are here somewhere, and I am going to find you. Find you and kill you, Ricky. Can you hear me, Ricky? Are you listening, Ricky?"

Ricky bends down to the ground. He feels around a bit and quietly picks up a good size branch, about eight inches long with some weight to it. He can see the assailant's silhouette from his vantage point, but he needs to be sure to get a kill shot and not start a gun battle. He throws the branch into a sparsely wooded, bushy area opposite the silhouette. When the branch lands, it shakes the undergrowth bushes as the thin branches snap. Dmitri opens fire into the bushy area where the branch had landed. As Dmitri is firing into the bushy undergrowth, Ricky opens fire on him, striking him with at least three shots. Dmitri stood still for a moment, and then he turns slowly in the direction of where Ricky is standing. Ricky is still deep in the shadows, and out of sight. Dmitri begins to raise his weapon, and then he falls to the ground.

During this time, the captain was calling Dmitri after trying and getting no response from Alex or Reko. When Dmitri too does not respond, the captain sends another car with four more Death Squad members to the site. Ricky takes a moment to collect his thoughts. He heads back toward the gate to leave the site. As he is closing the gate, he removes his lock and slips it into his pocket. Then he locks the chain with the original lock. He walks a few blocks from the site then he flags down a cab and takes off. Just in case he was being followed, he has the cab driver drop him several blocks from his apartment. Several minutes after Ricky had left the scene, the second car the captain had sent arrives at the site. They see the black Mercedes parked near the front gate. All four of the men get out of the car and approach the site gate, guns at the ready. They see the gate is chained and padlocked. One member takes out a gun and puts on a silencer. He shoots the padlock open. As he begins to remove the chain, two NYPD patrol cars on a routine patrol of the neighborhood stop at the scene.

"All right, all of you hold it right there," ordered an officer from the first car. The two officers from the second car come out of the car with shotguns in hand. They position themselves on the driver's side of the car for some additional protection, should there be a shootout. As the first two officers approach the men, the Death Squad member that shot open the padlock turns around, his gun still in his hand.

"Drop it! Don't do it!" the officer's shout out.

He ignores the warning, raises his weapon and fires a shot, missing the alert officers, and striking their car. The bullet shattered the front passenger window, and then it lodged itself in the windshield. The police return fire dropping him to the sidewalk. Seeing this unfold before their eyes, the other members draw out their firepower. The officer that was the first to approach was instantly shot in the chest. The shot sent him reeling backward and down to the ground into the street near his patrol car. The remaining three Patrolmen returned fire putting down the last three men. The two patrolmen with the shotguns observed the shooting aftermath. The four Death Squad members lie motionless on the sidewalk in front of the gate.

The other patrolman checks on his partner. He kneels down in the street next to the wounded officer and gently checks his vital signs. He was alive! The patrolman gets up and goes into the patrol car to call for an ambulance. He calls dispatch on the radio.

"Dispatch," the operator responds.

"This is Officer Steven Timmens, I have an officer down and I need an ambulance to 1201 Broadview Ave.

Stat! Notify the coroner's office as well, four passengers at the same address."

The operator asks, "Ours or theirs?"

Officer Timmens replies, "Theirs; please hurry with that ambulance."

"They're on their way, Officer, dispatch out."

An armed security team from the dept. of defense had also come out to investigate the gunfire. The police assured them that the situation is under control. The security team went back into their building. Meanwhile, unaware of the gun battle that had taken place at the site, Ricky stops by the twenty-four-hour post office. He places the package in his private P.O. box and then continues walking to his apartment.

Chapter 7

When Ricky gets home, he tells Sara about the events of the evening, "Sara, I think John may have been flipped."

"What," she exclaimed! "John, he would never!"

He was a little surprised by her reaction. "Sara, think about it, John tried to switch the plan three days ago and I scratched it. I go tonight and three guys show up to kill me!"

"What happened?"

"They all cashed out."

She just stares at him for a moment, and then she asks, "Did you get the package?"

"Yes, I got the package, and I stashed it. It's safe. I didn't want it here in the apartment."

"Why, why didn't you want it in the apartment?"

"It's not important, it's safe."

"Why won't you tell me? You do not trust me? You're running a deal, aren't you? You are cutting me out! I knew you would do this!"

"Listen, Sara, I told you before no deal. I am not cutting you out of anything."

"Ricky, how can we continue to work together without trust?"

"Listen to me, Sara, I still do not know who you talked to. I still do not understand why you were told that story. After this is finished, we will not have to work together again, ever. Someone put a contract out on me, was it John…or was it you, Sara?"

She flings her pearl white coffee mug at him. Missing him, it shatters behind him when it lands on the black and white marble floor in the foyer.

"You go to hell!"

She goes into the bedroom and slams the door. He goes into the kitchen and sits at the kitchen table trying to put the pieces together. *Who ordered the hit? Why did Sara react the way she did when I told her that I thought John had been flipped by the U.S. Why did she just stare at me when I told her that the assassins cashed out? Or the fact that John's number was not on her phone and he said he has never spoken with her. So, who if anyone, called her? Where did this story come from? I will get up early tomorrow, go get the package, bring it to the captain, and then with or without the payoff, one way or another, I will disappear.* He goes into the living room, lies down on the sofa to go to sleep, and places his gun under the pillow. He falls asleep and wakes up around seven a.m. He sits up, rubs his eyes, and sees Sara is standing in front of him, fully dressed.

He looks up at her. "What are you doing, are you going to work now, this early?"

"No, I am going with you."

"Going with me, where? What do you mean?"

"I mean I am going with you to get the package and we are going to see the captain. If John did his job correctly, when we deliver the package, we will collect the attaché case you spoke of. Then we will split up the money and then we split from each other."

"Sara, stop, what I told you was hearsay, I don't know for sure there will be any attaché."

"You are a liar!"

"I am not lying; I know upon successful completion we are going to be compensated. I also told you that sometimes compensation is an execution. Also hearsay, but that's part of the risk."

"I don't care, get dressed. We are doing this together."

She goes into the kitchen to make a cup of coffee. He gets up, grabs his gun, and goes into the bedroom to change his clothes. Once again, he puts on the shoulder holster because he feels now, this mission could go wrong in a couple of ways. The way Sara has been acting she's probably heavy too. He comes out of the bedroom ready to go. Sara is waiting in the foyer by the apartment door. At around this same time, a police investigation is underway at the site. They determined as they wore the same uniforms that this was an internal thing, a deal gone bad, internal execution. They believe the three men found on the property, were killed by the same four men that were slain in the gun battle with the police the night before. A piece of material was discovered, stuck on the gate. It matched the torn sleeve of one of the victims indicating they probably climbed over the gate to evade their pursuers. They were not able to identify the men. They called in the FBI because these uniforms in the photos looked like paramilitary. The FBI has access to more data. They could only identify them as being members of the Russian underground. The men had no I.D.'s on them of any type. They were identified only by the insignia patch on their shirts. The FBI stated this case is now officially closed.

The officer that had been shot, Billy Laiman, survived thanks to his body armor. When he was released from the hospital, he retired from the force. "Alright Sara, if you insist, let's get going."

She nods and they leave the apartment. Sara walks out to the street to flag down a cab and Ricky tells her, "Forget the cab, we are walking."

"Walking, why, are we walking?"

"Do you want to get the package?"

"Yes."

"Then we are walking, follow me."

"Where are we going, Ricky?"

"We're going to the post office."

"Do you need to mail a letter?"

"No, I am picking up the package."

"You mailed the package to yourself?"

"No, come on, we're almost there."

They arrive at the post office and go inside. Ricky goes over to the P.O. box section and he gets the package.

"Oh, I see, this is where you kept it. Why wouldn't you tell me last night?"

"It doesn't matter, let's go."

They leave and start walking up the street. At one point while walking, as they are passing an alley, Sara stumbles and falls into Ricky and pushes him into the alley. As he helps her up, she faces him and hits him in the chest with a stun gun, he drops to the pavement. She grabs the package and his gun then exits the alley while he is still immobilized.

She walks up the block back to the apartment. She goes upstairs and stows away the package and his gun.

She goes back downstairs, jumps in a cab, and takes off. After a while, he awakes from being stunned. He does a quick check and finds that the package and his gun are gone. He has nothing. No way to protect himself, and nothing to bring to the captain. He gets up, still shaking off the effects of the stun gun. He's not sure what to do. His head is spinning just thinking that Sara has been behind all of this. *She made up the story about John and me running a private deal, the hitmen, all of it, Sara? Maybe she took the package to the captain for the payoff so there would be no split or maybe she's gone rogue. Maybe she has had a private buyer all along. I'm calling John.*

"Hello?"

"John, it's Ricky."

"Hello, Ricky, what can I do for you?"

"Someone has been flipped and I believe it is Sara."

"Sara, what do you mean?"

"The night I picked up the package three Russian Death Squad guys arrived at the site to kill me."

"What did you say?"

"You heard me."

"What happened, wait, let me guess, did they cash out?"

"Yes, they did, and when I got home and told Sara she flipped out."

"Well sure, if you are right about her and she ordered the hit."

"When you returned home, she knew her plan had failed. You see, if she gets you out the way after you have the package, then they would have taken the package from

93

you and deliver it to her. When you cashed them out you ruined her plan, if, in fact, it was her plan."

"You know, John, that's what I've been thinking. Due to how she has been acting lately. That is why I decided to stash the package."

"I would go and retrieve it in the morning and complete the mission."

"Yes, and in doing so you would have cut her out."

"I was not thinking about cutting her out, we are partners."

"Come on, Ricky, you know better than that. You never know who you can trust in this business."

"Yes, I know."

"So, what happened?"

"This morning when I woke up, she was standing right in front of me. She was fully dressed and ready to go."

"Go, go where?"

"Go with me to get the package."

"Go on."

"I got dressed and we left the building. We walked to the post office, that's where I kept it. I got the package and we left the post office. We were walking up the street when she stumbled into me and pushed me into an alley we were passing. When I helped her up, she hit me in the chest with a Stun gun. She took the package and my gun."

"Sara did this?"

"Yes, now I don't know what to do, I have nothing to deliver and still need to report to the captain."

"Well you know, Ricky, if you run, they will find you and that will be worse, much worse."

"So, what are you saying?"

"I am saying, go see the captain, tell him your story then show him the Stun gun burn marks. Maybe he will let you go. I will vouch for you. Tell the captain to call me, I have to go now."

"Thanks, John."

Ricky brushes himself off and walks up the street.

He stops in a deli and gets a cup of coffee. He knew that he really needed the payoff, now he hopes he can just walk away alive. He gets a cab and he goes downtown. He tells the driver, "Washington Square Park, near the arch."

He arrives, pays the driver, and starts walking to his meeting. He gets to the building, goes down the stairs and he sees crime scene tape sealing off the door. He knocks on the door anyway. No one answers so he knocks again louder, still nothing. A man leans over the railing and calls down to him, "Hey, what are you doing down there? They are all gone."

"Gone, who, what do you mean, who are you?"

"I'm the building manager; do you know these people, were they friends of yours?"

"No, I, uh, I answered an ad, I was looking for work."

"Well, I don't know what kind of job they were offering, they were all arrested by the police. The feds showed up too."

"The feds, are you sure?"

"Yep, someone reported gunfire and the police swarmed the place. Yeah, the report was they killed some woman right there in the basement."

Ricky stares up at the man in disbelief, and he has no words. He looks down and thinks, *Oh no, was it Sara?*

"I think you must be at the wrong address."

The man leaves and Ricky sits on the metal stairs. With his head in his hands, trying take in what he had just heard. *Could it be it was Sara, he was referring to? If she came here to make the exchange, did something go wrong? If she gave them the package and it was correct, why would they kill her? Did she try to negotiate the payoff? I have to get out of here. I need to find out what happened.*

He runs up the stairs and then starts walking up the street toward the park. He takes his phone and calls John, "Hello?"

"Hello, John, it's Ricky."

"Hello, Ricky, what's up, how did your meeting go?"

"I mean you are calling me so he did not kill you, so how did it go?"

"I don't really know what to make of it, John. I went to see the captain and when I arrived no one was there."

"What do you mean?"

"Just what I said, I knocked several times. There was crime scene tape on the door and no response."

"Crime scene tape, what did you do?"

"Nothing, while I was banging on the door a man leaned over the railing and told me they were all arrested."

"What man; arrested, by whom, and for what?"

"He said he was the building manager. He told me gunfire was reported from down in the basement and the police and the feds took them all away. He said he heard they had killed a woman."

"Was it Sara?"

"I don't know yet. I need you to make some calls and get back to me right away, please."

"Okay, Ricky, okay, I will get back to you. What are you going to do in the meantime?"

"I don't know John. I really don't know. The package is gone, Sara is gone, and the mission is over. See what you can find out and let me know, thanks."

Ricky continues walking up the street and when he gets to the park, he sits down on a bench to try to sort things out. *The plan was going so well and now nothing makes any sense. Who was killed if anyone, and was it Sara? What happened to the package, and my gun?*

Who called the police, and why were the feds called in? I understand that if gunfire was heard, the police would be called in, but why the feds? With the exception of a woman being killed, this plays out exactly like the story Sara said she was told about what I had done. Maybe John will learn something. He gets up and walks out of the park. He flags down a cab and heads to the apartment. He arrives and goes up to the apartment, no one is there. He takes a shower and he looks at the Stun gun burn marks on his chest. He finishes up and as he is getting changed.

He gets a call from John, "Hello, John."

"Yes Ricky, this is what I learned. There are no reports of gunfire and no record, local or federal, of any arrests at that address today."

"What did you say?"

"That's right, you are still being played by someone. I also learned that they moved their operation two days ago."

"Really, and no one told me, how was I to complete the mission if could not drop off the package?"

"This I do not know; you should have been contacted. Ricky, you really need to be careful, do you have another weapon?"

"Yes."

"Keep it with you, and Ricky."

"Yes?"

"If someone is near you and they stumble, step out the way. Good luck."

"Thanks John."

Ricky goes into the bedroom to get another weapon. Now he will wait to see what happens. He did not have to wait very long. His phone rings, he looks at the screen, it's Sara. "Hello, Sara, are you alright? Where are y—"

"No Ricky, not Sara, it is Captain Yurjinsky."

"Yes, Captain, sorry, my phone must have a malfunction. The name on the screen is Sara."

"I know, Ricky, this is her phone. She is here with us now."

"Tell me why you did not deliver the package?"

"I do not have the package."

"Why did you fail to complete the mission?"

"No, you do not understand, Captain. I completed the mission. I was on my way to bring it to you this morning."

"You never arrived, why?"

"Sara took the package from me."

"What, how could she have taken the package from you, were you careless with it?"

"No sir."

"Then explain!"

"I woke up early this morning to bring the package directly to you. Sara was waiting to go with me. After I got

98

the package the other night, I stored it in a P.O. box for safety."

"Why did you not keep it with you?"

"Sara had been displaying unusual behavior and I felt uneasy about having it in the apartment. So, we went to the post office this morning to get the package, and we started on our way to see you. At one point on the walk, she stumbled into me and we fell into an alleyway. When I helped her up, she hit me in the chest with a stun gun. It knocked me out cold and when I came to my senses; both the package and my gun were gone."

"Sara did this to you?"

"Yes sir."

"If you were unconscious, how do you know it was Sara that took everything, it could have been anyone."

"Why else would she do what she did if not to take the package and deliver to you herself?"

"Ricky, Sara does not have the package. She told us you have it, and you are making a private deal. Believe me, we interrogated her, thoroughly."

"Captain, I am telling you what happened, she could have stashed that package anywhere. She may have already made the deal."

"Ricky, you need to come here now."

"Where? I went to your command center earlier, no one was there, and it's a crime scene. Are you there now?"

"We had to move to a new location, surely Sara told you this."

"No sir, she did not. I went to the command center where we met last time."

"She did not tell you or send you a text message?"

"No sir, you have her phone, see for yourself. What is the new location address?"

"777 6th Ave, walk around to the back of the building, then you will find the stairs to the basement. I will expect you soon."

Ricky grabs a black sports jacket to conceal his weapon and heads downstairs to get a cab. When he reaches the lobby, he runs into Al and Alice.

"Hey, Ricky, how's it going?" Al asks?

"Oh, hey, Al, hello, Alice, fine, everything is fine."

"So, where is that lovely Sara," Alice asks?

"Sara, oh, she is out of town for a while, family thing."

"Oh, is everything alright?"

"Yes, I believe so, Alice."

"You didn't want to go with her?"

"I wanted to Alice but I could not get away. If you both will please excuse me, I am late for an important appointment."

"Sure Ricky, no problem. Good to see you again, stop by sometime."

"Yes, yes, I uh, we will, thanks."

"We hope everything is okay, regards to Sara," Alice adds.

With that, they go up to their apartment and Ricky leaves and gets a cab to go to the meeting. He arrives at the address he was given. He walks around to the back of the building and finds the stairs. He walks down the stairs and knocks on the large black metal door.

"What do you want?" a big, gruff voice asks from behind the door.

"It's Ricky. I am here to see the captain."

The door opens and he is grabbed on the arm by someone and he is pulled into the room. The large steel door slams shut behind him. The room is pitch dark, and silent. In the blackness, he is grabbed and held on each arm by two large men. Other hands frantically grab at Ricky's jacket and clothing. They find and take away his weapon.

"Hello?" Ricky calls out inquisitively.

A single voice responds through the darkness, "Hello, Ricky."

Then, a small lamp is switched on. In the dim light, he sees the captain sitting at an old brown wooden desk. "Hello, Captain."

"Do you have the package, Ricky?"

"No sir, I told you on the phone what happened."

Another dim overhead lamp is switched on. He now sees several large men in the room, and they are armed. Then a third light is switched on and he sees Sara. She has been severely beaten and she is tied to a chair and her mouth is duct-taped shut.

"What happened here, Captain, who did this to her?"

"You, arrogant bastard," the captain yells! "You come to me with nothing after another week, and you are going to question me on what happened to her! For your information, it was only after we beat her when she finally confessed that you made a deal for cash. That you sold my package!"

"No sir, it happened just as I told you. I had the package but it was taken from me."

He reaches under his jacket and all guns draw down on him. He tells them, "Please, relax; I am just opening my shirt."

He unbuttons his shirt to reveal the stun gun burn marks. "Captain, please take a look for yourself."

The captain gets up and approaches him. He takes a flashlight and examines the marks. "I see, these are stun gun burns, kill her."

The men turn and raise their weapons to shoot and kill Sara and Ricky yells, "Stop!"

The captain turns to him, "Stop, why Ricky? Did you not just proclaim her to be a traitor, and further prove it with those burn marks?"

"Well, yes but…"

"But what?"

Taking out his own weapon, a forty-five-caliber pistol, he points the barrel at Ricky's forehead, "Either she is lying or it is you!"

"Captain, you must listen to me, please. I do not have your package, and you do not have your package. She may be the only one that knows where the package is. If you shoot her all is lost."

The captain thinks for a moment. He Holsters his gun and orders the men to shoulder their weapons. He looks at Sara then turns to Ricky, "Ricky, I want that package. If she will not lead us to it, I will have no choice."

"No choice, sir?"

"I will allow this to play out for only a short time. If I do not get the package, I will have no use for either of you. I will contact John and tell him to do it again. Different agents will be sent to retrieve a new package as both of you will be retired. Do you understand?"

"Yes sir."

"I do not understand you, Ricky. You claim this woman knocked you out, robbed you. Then she gave you up, and yet you want her to live. I must admit I find this behavior a little peculiar."

He turns to his men and barks out, "Wake her!"

One man walks over to Sara and he wakes her up by ripping the tape off of her mouth. She is bleeding from her mouth and areas of her face where the skin was damaged by the tape. She is so weak from a lack of food or water she barely makes a sound. The captain walks over to her, and grabs her by her hair, and pulls her head up. Her body is full of pain and her heart is full of anger. "Hello, Sara, Sara, wake up we need to talk."

She slightly opens her left eye. The right eye is black and blue, and swollen shut. "Now Sara, Ricky is here. He said you used a stun gun on him, and took the package. Is this true?"

She looks across and sees Ricky. They have him seated and taped to a chair with two armed men standing beside him. She lets her head droop down and she begins to weep gently. Then in a low, raspy voice, she tells the captain, "Alright, no more. If you will untie me, let me get cleaned up, and tend to my wounds, I will take you to get your package."

"Good, very good, boys untie her and let her go fix herself."

They remove her bonds. She tries to get up out of the chair. She had been there for hours and she had a hard time moving her legs. They had beaten her arms and legs, they were badly bruised. Ricky offers to help her and the captain looks at him. "You now want to help her?"

Ricky thinks for a moment before he answers. "No sir, I want to help you. Helping her get right is helping you. Unless your men want to do it."

The captain looks around at his men and they all turn away. "Alright, Ricky, you may help her. My men will keep their weapons trained on both of you. If you try anything, neither of you will leave this room alive. Cut him loose now, and watch them both."

Chapter 8

Ricky goes over to help Sara. He cannot believe how they had beaten her. As mad as he was at her for what she did to him, he now wants to kill the captain and his crew. However, he knows this is not the time. He helps her up and he walks her slowly to the bathroom. He turns to the captain, "Excuse me, sir, I will need ice, clean bandages, and a cane."

"She needs a cane?"

"Yes sir, she really is having a hard time standing, or walking."

The captain has one of the men run out to get the items. Ricky continues to help clean her up. He finds some antiseptic cleanser in the medicine cabinet, and begins to apply some to her wounds. A short while later the guard returns with the requested items. He gives the items to Ricky. It takes about an hour or so for Ricky to get Sara to a point where she can be moved. She looks at the captain, and still in a strained voice, "Okay, let's go get this over with."

They leave the basement and start to make their way up the stairs. It is a long, tedious, and painful walk going up the stairs for Sara. Ricky helps her reach the top of the stairs and they begin to walk around to the front of the building. The others go ahead to bring the cars around to pick them up. The captain waits with them and says, "You two will ride with me and my driver. The others will follow right behind."

The cars pull up and they get in. "Okay, where to, the captain asks?"

Sara tells him, "Go to Riverside Park."

"What address, what street!"

"79th and Riverside Drive." Ricky looks at her; he knows that is their building but he does not say a word. He has no idea what she is doing but if she is playing them, he knows they are dead. They arrive and the four of them go into the building. The other four guards remain outside in their car and wait. Charles, the doorman sees them come in and sees Sara come in all bandaged and bruised.

"Excuse Mrs. Rogers, what happened, do you need medical attention?"

Sara looks at Ricky to answer, "No, Charles, thank you, we just came from the medical center. She was in an accident, she just needs to go upstairs and get some rest."

"Okay Mr. Rogers, are these gentlemen with you, sir?"

"Yes, yes, they are, Charles."

"Alright sir, please call me if you need any help with Mrs. Rogers."

"Thanks, Charles." They walk over to the elevators and go upstairs. They go into the apartment and Sara starts to vomit. Ricky takes in her into the bathroom.

Once inside she whispers to him, "We will use the listening device special keywords like secret laser data, weapons, and armed men to bring the watchers in. Draw their attention to the armed men in the car downstairs and say something to get the authorities across the street up here. Now we are no longer spies but hostages."

"Fine, okay I will, but tell me is the package here?"

"Yes, I will get it, you do your part."

The captain bangs on the door, "Hey what are you doing in there? Open this door, now!"

Ricky opens the door and they exit. "Where is my package, my patience is wearing thin!"

She looks at him, coldly, still only able to open her left eye. "I will go get it now."

Sara starts to make her way slowly toward the bedroom clutching onto her cane.

"So, Ricky, you are married, now I understand why you want to help her even though she turned on you."

Ricky looks at him. "Captain, we are not married, it is an illusion."

"An illusion, what do you mean?"

"It is part of our cover, as far as anyone knows we are married. What about the other four-armed men downstairs in front of the building waiting in the car?"

"What about them? They are of no concern to you. They will come if I call them. Where is she with the package?"

"I am sorry, Captain, but she can barely move after the beating your men gave her. You almost beat her to death."

"She got what she deserved, no one steals from me."

"I can't believe that you would have beaten her so severely over something like the secret plans of the U.S. laser data you had acquired."

"I have still not acquired it and if it is not in my hands in one minute, I will kill both of you. I will bring my men up from outside and we will take this place apart."

"Okay, let me see what's taking so long."

Ricky heads to the bedroom and the captain sends his driver, Carl, with him. Sara asks for help because she cannot walk. Ricky and Carl go to help her. As they do, she slips a small Glock 43 gun into Ricky's right-hand sports jacket pocket, and then she hits Carl with her stun gun. He falls to the floor and Ricky grabs his gun.

The captain yells out, "Well, where is my package!"

Ricky and Sara come into the living room.

"Where's my driver, Carl?"

"Captain, he is in the bathroom."

"Fine, is that my package?"

"Yes, here is your package of U.S. laser data." She tosses at him.

"Good, very good, now there are just a couple of loose ends to take care of. Carl, Carl," he yells! "What are you doing in there? We have to finish and go come on, Carl?"

Carl does not respond and the captain takes out his gun. "What happened to my driver, Carl? Speak!"

"Captain Yurjinsky, what are you going to do with that gun? You have the package, now go."

The keywords used by Ricky activate the device and the watchers began to move into action. They quickly notify the NYPD and the area FBI agents to go to the address. The FBI agents go to the address and they know to stand down and let the NYPD handle the situation. The agents were made aware of a secret deal that was already in place with Sara and hopefully, Ricky. Meanwhile, back in the apartment...

"Go!" the captain shouts, "I'm not going anywhere! Carl, Carl!"

He leaves them standing in the living room while he goes into the bedroom to find Carl. He knows that they cannot run. Sara can barely move. He finds Carl lying on the floor in the bedroom. He walks back into the living room. "What did you do to Carl?"

They both stare at him in silence. "Well, it does not matter really. Now it looks like I will just have to kill you both myself, say goodbye to each other."

He raises his gun toward them, and then takes out his phone to call the others to come up and help with Carl. While waiting for his men to respond he looks at Ricky. "You know, Ricky, I am surprised that after all of this you remain content to allow your wife to suffer like this."

His men do not respond. "I think you should suffer as much as she has. Since I can no longer bear watch her standing there half-blind and in excruciating pain, I will shoot her first so you can watch her die. Then, after you have had a moment or two to suffer her loss, I will kill you."

He tries again to reach his men and still no response. He looks angrily at Ricky and Sara, then he bellows, "What did you do with my men?"

They both just stare at him, not saying a word. Leveling his gun at them he asks again even louder, "What did you do with my men?"

A gunshot rings out. The captain stares at them then looks at his gun. He did not fire his weapon. He winces a bit, and raises his gun toward them again, when a second shot rings out, he collapses to the floor. About now is when Carl begins to come around from being knocked cold. He comes out of the bedroom still a little dazed and he sees the captain on the floor lying in a pool of blood.

He screams out in Russian at Ricky and Sara. He quickly bends to grab the captain's bloodied pistol. As Carl was rising up, and begins to turn toward them. Another shot rings out striking him in the head and he falls to the floor next to the captain's lifeless body. Moments after the shooting, Ricky looks down and sees that Sara had slipped her hand into his sports jacket pocket and shot them both right from inside the jacket pocket.

She tells Ricky with a strained voice to, "Go and get the package, and I owe you a jacket."

He walks over and bends down to pick up the blood-splattered package lying near the captain's body. He goes into the kitchen and rinses the package off. He stashes it in the back of a high cabinet in the kitchen. He turns and goes back into the living room and takes hold of her to help her stand. Suddenly, a loud knock on the door shatters the violent aftermath of silence in the room.

Chapter 9

"Mr. and Mrs. Rogers, it's Charles, the doorman. Is everything alright, hello?"

"Charles, thank God, please, get the police, and please call an ambulance for Mrs. Rogers."

"Yes sir, Mr. Rogers."

About five minutes later there was another knock on the door.

"Mr. Rogers," a voice yells through the door, "NYPD."

"The door is open, Officer, please come in."

The police enter the apartment, led by Lieutenant Bill Williams.

Ricky calls out, "We're in the living room."

The lieutenant walks in first with eight other officers walking through the apartment to secure the area. He sees Ricky holding on to Sara and the two bodies on the floor.

"I'm Lieutenant Williams of the NYPD, are you Mr. Rogers?"

"Yes, I'm Ricky Rogers."

"We apprehended four armed men that were waiting in a car in front of the building on a tip we received. I take it they were waiting for these two. The doorman came outside and told us you had some trouble. After talking with him, we came up to your apartment. The FBI is standing by if needed. Right now, this is our jurisdiction. Would you care to tell me just what happened here?"

"Yes Lieutenant, but right now I need to get my wife to the hospital. The ambulance has just arrived. The EMTs will be up here at any moment. Once they have her secure and on her way to the hospital, we will talk, please?"

"Yes, yes of course, what happened to her?"

Ricky points down at the floor, "Them, they did this to her. Them and the other four."

"Why?"

"What else, money."

"Money, what do you mean?"

"They abducted my wife. She left for work but she never got there."

"How do you know she did not get there? Did her office call you and ask for her?"

"No, not at all, I became aware of this only this afternoon. Here, check my phone."

Lieutenant Williams views the call log. "Yes, I see the last inbound call was from a Sara, so?"

"It was not Sara, it was only Sara's phone, and that man right there called, pointing to the captain. He told me they had Sara and wanted me to bring them two million dollars if I want to get my wife back. He gave me the address of where I was to meet them, 777 6th Ave. the basement entrance around the back of the building."

"Alright Mr. Rogers, I will send some of my men to check it out, Sergeant."

"Yes sir. Take a few men with you and go check this address out. We're just going to continue to sort things out

112

here. I mean, I still have two dead guys to account for. Get back to me right away."

"Yes sir," the sergeant replied.

"So, tell me, what did you do, Mr. Rogers?"

"Well, I did not have the ransom amount, but I decided to go and get Sara anyway."

"Okay, tell me how you were going to do that?"

"I did not know, but I knew I was going to get her away from them somehow."

"Please, continue."

"Well, I went to the address he gave me."

"When I arrived, I went around to the back of the building and went down the stairs. I knocked on the door and when it opened, I was grabbed, and pulled into a pitch-dark room."

"Then what happened?"

"They began turning on some lights and that is when I saw Sara tied to a chair and beaten. I was asked for the money and told them I did not have it. The leader, pointing down again to the captain's body, ordered the other men to shoot Sara."

"I told them if they do not kill her and let me tend to her, we will all go to our apartment. I told him we have hundreds of thousands of dollars' worth of jewelry and transferrable bearer bonds. I will give them all that we have."

"So, what happened after you made the offer?"

"Sara had passed out and he had one of his men awaken her by ripping the large piece of grey duct tape away from her face and mouth. He allowed me to tend to her a bit then we left and came here. Sara and I rode with these two and the other four followed behind us to our apartment."

"I'm curious, Mr. Rogers, seeing your wife so badly hurt and beaten, why didn't you insist on an ambulance?"

"Lieutenant Williams, please, these men were only moments away from killing her right in front of me. They would have never allowed an ambulance."

"Okay, tell me what happened when you had arrived at home?"

"We entered the lobby and were greeted as usual by Charles, the doorman, he noticed Sara's injuries. I told him she was in an accident and we had just come from the medical center. In retrospect, I don't think Charles really believed me. Like when he asked about these two men that were with us."

"What did he ask you?"

"He asked me if they were with us."

"What did you tell him?"

"I told him they were and when I did, Charles just looked at me and nodded. As we made our way to the elevator, Charles called out, 'Mr. Rogers, if you need any help with Mrs. Rogers please let me know, anything.'

"I thanked him, and then we entered the elevator and went up to our apartment."

"What happened once you were inside?"

"They had us stand in the living room."

"Stand, you mean they wouldn't let your wife sit down?"

"No sir, while we stood there he had his driver, I believe his name was Carl, start to look through the apartment for the jewels and bonds I spoke of. He found nothing. With that, the leader turned to Sara and me and brandished his weapon. He ordered us to produce the items."

"What did you do?"

"I helped Sara into the bedroom to get them what they wanted. While we were in there, Sara went into the closet, but instead of getting the jewels and bonds she instead grabbed the stun gun and a real gun."

"A gun, you have guns in this apartment?"

"Yes sir, fully licensed and registered, we both do."

"Why is that exactly, target shooting?"

"Well, yes, but both of us have licenses due to our work."

"Your work what kind of work?"

"I have an office on Park Avenue and I handle large commercial real estate and government accounts. Sometimes I have large amounts of cash, and Sara is a lawyer."

"Your wife is a lawyer?"

"Yes."

"Okay, Mr. Rogers, please, continue."

"When we were exiting the bedroom, she slipped the gun into my jacket pocket and then she said to Carl, 'Help me, he can't do it alone.' Carl stepped in to support her from the right side. As he did, she zapped him with the stun gun and he went down."

"What happened then, Mr. Rogers, how did these two guys get dead?"

"We exited the bedroom and were asked at gunpoint, 'where is Carl?'

"I told him he was using the bathroom. He then asked, 'Where is the merchandise.'

"Sara just ogled him with contempt in her eye. Again, he demanded, 'Where is the merchandise!'

"With still no response, he yelled, 'Liars!'"

"He raised his gun and said, 'That's enough' and a shot rang out, then another."

"He fired at you?"

"I didn't know at first, I looked at Sara and she had not been hit, I felt around I was not hit either. Then I looked back toward the captain and he was on his knees, then he went face down as you see him there."

"Okay, what about the other guy?"

"He came to and he came out of the bedroom still dazed from being stunned."

"When he saw the scene in the living room, he started screaming at us in Russian or at least it sounded like Russian. He came at us after picking up the captain's gun and Sara shot him as well."

"She told me he was the primary guy that beat her. Do you have any further questions for me, Lieutenant?"

"No, that explains it along with the doorman's testimony I think we're done here. I will report what you told me and the shooting's will be written as self-defense."

"Thank you, Lieutenant Williams."

The lieutenant's phone rings; it was the sergeant. "Lieutenant, this place checks out just like he said."

"Okay great, Sergeant, gather up any evidence that pertains to this mess and bring it to me so we can bag and tag it all."

"Yes sir, Lieutenant, will do."

"That was the report on the address you gave us. Everything checks out. I will call the coroner and have these guys removed."

"Thanks again, Lieutenant, will there be anything else?"

"Not at this time. We will call you if we need anything more. Why don't you go see your wife? I'll stick around here and wait for the coroner."

"Okay, yes, thank you. I am going there now."

When Ricky gets down to the lobby, he sees Charles. "Hello, Charles, thank you so much for your help this evening."

"My pleasure, Mr. Rogers, I didn't want to say anything when you came in but I did not think those guys were with you."

"Good eye, Charles, and thanks again. I'm on my way now to see Sara, uh Mrs. Rogers in the hospital."

"Okay, goodnight, Mr. Rogers. I hope Mrs. Rogers is feeling better, see you tomorrow."

"Goodnight, Charles."

Ricky went out and grabbed a cab over to Cornell Medical Center where the ambulance had taken her. When he arrives at the hospital, he checks in at the reception desk. The nurse on duty tells him that she is on the third floor, room 305. He walks over to the elevators and goes up to her room. When he enters the room, he is pleasantly surprised to see that she looks better. "Hello, Sara."

"Hi," she replies weakly. "You are looking a bit better; they got almost all of the swelling gone from around your eye. What did they say about your arms and legs?"

"They are not broken just bruised; it's the same with my arms. It will take a little time but they tell me this will all heal."

A nurse comes into the room; it's time to give Sara something for the pain. "I know you need your rest now, Sara, so I'm going to leave. I will be back tomorrow to see how you're doing and find out how much longer you will be here."

"Thank you, Ricky," she whispers. "When I get home, I will have a lot to tell you."

He smiles. "Good, yes, we have a lot to discuss."

Then he leans in and kisses her on the forehead. "Goodnight Sara, see you tomorrow."

He makes his way out of the hospital, gets a cab, and heads home. He arrives and goes up to his apartment. He enters, and everyone has gone. Only the terribly blood-stained carpet remained. He looks around and realizes he cannot stay there tonight. He quickly packs a few things and leaves the apartment. He checks in to the Riverside Towers hotel. It is about a block away from his building. The next morning, he calls a cleaning service to have the apartment cleaned. He tells them about the bloodstains to be removed. He also calls the front desk in his building to authorize access for the cleaning service. Then he calls his office and reschedules all of his appointments to the next day. He leaves the hotel and is on his way to the hospital when he gets a call, "Hello?"

"Hello, Mr. Rogers, it is Lieutenant Williams."

"Hello, sir, what can I do for you?"

"First off, how's your wife doing?"

"Good, you know, as good as can be expected. No broken bones and they were able to save her right eye."

"That's good to hear. I have some information for you, Mr. Rogers."

"Yes?"

"We were able to establish the I.D. of one of the two men from the apartment. They were bad men, Mr. Rogers, real bad men. You are both very lucky to be alive."

"Why, who were they?"

"They were part of the Russian underground."

"The Russian underground, what is the Russian underground?"

"It's a group of military personnel of varying ranks that became disgruntled with the status quo. They have their own agendas, and they have gone rogue. Nothing they do is sanctioned by anyone, and nothing they do is legal."

"These were the men in my apartment?"

"Yes sir, we found a list of suspected crimes working with the FBI. Alleged executions and multiple other things like espionage and abductions. All of the murder victims, for the most part, at one time were members or operatives of the underground. That was until for some reason they would become persona non grata with the underground. The leader as you called him was in fact a leader. He held the rank of captain. His name was Ben Yurjinsky. He was in the Russian military before he went rogue. He was into a lot of real bad stuff. Abductions, like the way they took your wife. More than fifty victims, all were women. Unfortunately, none of the others fared as well as your wife. Well, I thought you might like to know how lucky you both are. Take care of yourself, Mr. Rogers, and take care of your wife."

"Thank you, Lieutenant Williams, I will."

Chapter 10

He sits quietly in the back of the cab and shifts his focus to Sara. When he arrives at the hospital, he stops in the gift shop. He purchases some flowers for her. He buys her roses, red roses. He leaves the gift shop, and walks around the lobby down the hall to the elevators. He goes up to the third floor, and he enters her room. "Hello, Sara, how are you feeling? Hey, you look great."

"I'm doing okay, the doctors here are wonderful."

He hands her the flowers. "They are beautiful, thank you, here." She hands them back to him. "Please, set them in the water pitcher for now."

"Sure, let me have them. What did the doctor say?"

"He said if I want to go home, they could discharge me. Do you want me to come home, Ricky?"

"Well, if you're really up to it, then I think it would best."

"I had the whole place cleaned, scrubbed, and fumigated. I replaced anything that could not be saved. So yeah, let's go home, we have a lot of catching up to do."

"Yes, we do. I have been waiting to talk with you. Listen, it's all good."

"All right, you call for the discharge nurse and have her bring you out to the cabstand. I will go get in line for a cab."

Sara calls for the nurse and she comes into her room with a wheelchair. The nurse helps Sara into the wheelchair. Then she brings her down to the waiting area while they complete the discharge process. The cabstand is where the cabs pick up passengers leaving the hospital. The nurse brings Sara out of the hospital. Ricky sees them and waves and the nurse brings her over to him. They all wait together until a cab arrives. Sara needs to ride upfront because it easier access than the back seat, and there was more legroom. Ricky gets into the back seat and they head back to their apartment. When they arrive, Charles, the doorman, goes out to meet them at the curb. Ricky exits the cab first.

"Hello, Charles, thanks for coming out to help and thanks again for all your help the other night."

"It's my pleasure, Mr. Rogers, hey, hold on just a minute."

Charles turns and runs back into the building. Moments later, he reappears with a wheelchair. Ricky is watching and sees Charles come out of the building with a wheelchair, "Charles, you are a wonder."

"Thanks Mr. Rogers, I bought this myself. I keep it in the backroom, you know, just in case."

"Well, I for one am grateful Charles, how about helping me get my wife out of the car?"

"Sure."

They open the door and help Sara out of the car. Sara graciously accepts the offer of a wheelchair. Ricky pays the cab driver. They all go into the building and up to the apartment. They go inside and the place is perfect like nothing happened. Sara gets up out of the wheelchair and thanks Charles. Ricky takes care of him and thanks him again. Sara very slowly makes her way around the living room.

She turns and looks at Ricky, "I am ready to talk if you are ready to listen."

"Do you want to sit down, Sara?"

"No, I need to use my legs, I will stand. You can sit down and make yourself comfortable if you want."

He walks over and sits on the sofa. "Okay, ready when you are, Sara."

"Ricky, I'm sure you have many questions about how things went down, don't you?"

"Yes, as a matter of fact I do."

"I know I was caught in a game and I wasn't a player. Why don't we start there?"

"All right, here goes. The Death Squad guys that showed up at the site, Yurjinsky ordered it. He found out the date and time of the pick-up. He got it on one of his update calls with John."

"How do you know this to be true?"

"I called John, the real John, here."

She hands her phone to him; he checks the log and John's number was there. "So, what did John say exactly?"

"He said the captain called and demanded a progress update and the expected delivery date. So, John told him."

"All right, that explains that. He sends the messengers to take me out, recover the package and bring it to him, no cash payoff. He was a miserable bastard."

"You know, I have another big question, why did you hit me with your stun gun?"

122

"Okay, it's like this, do you remember when you came back to the apartment after the incident at the site?"

"Yes, that was not a very good night."

"You came in and said you thought John may have been flipped by the U.S."

"Yeah, and you reacted oddly at the news I thought."

"I did, yes, and that is why I had to use the stun gun. I didn't know what else to do. I mean, I didn't want to shoot you. You are very good at your job and you were getting too close."

"Too close, Sara, too close to what?"

"Well, you see, Ricky, things are not as they seem."

"What do you mean?"

"When you came home that night and said you thought John had been flipped, I freaked out because I...I have been flipped."

He stares at her for a brief moment. "You have been flipped, what?"

"What are you saying, Sara?"

"Listen, Ricky, let me tell you. We said we were doing this mission for a big payoff and we said we're getting out, isn't that what we agreed?"

"Yes, that's what we said, but there is no big payoff."

"Ricky, let me finish. I needed to get my hands on the package to ensure it did not make its way to the captain."

"What are you talking about? You insisted on it going to the captain. Did you forget your own words?"

"No, just hear me out."

"Sara, this is crazy talk, but sure, please continue."

"I was approached and was offered a deal to get rid of Captain Yurjinsky, recover and return the package to them."

"A deal, who offered you a deal, and for what?"

"The FBI, they said if I can achieve these goals, I will have purchased our freedom."

"And if you fail to achieve the goals, then what?"

"Then, if we were still alive, we would both be arrested and tried as spies. We will be prosecuted, and sent to prison, Federal Prison."

"So, you decided to take on the captain and his crew by yourself, impressive, risky, but very impressive. Why did you decide to go it alone?"

"I had to somehow get him to come here, you know, convince him that we had the package and I just wanted to see the big payoff cash."

"Then I would have them bring me here to get the package and I would have a chance to kill him."

"What did the captain say?"

"He said nothing; he just had one of the guards punch me in the face, my right eye, his driver Carl did it."

"Well, it sounded like a good plan going in."

"Thanks, but to be honest, I did not figure on all of the beatings, that part was rough. I knew I would not be able to do anything to Yurjinsky on his home field. So, I told them you had the package and an interested buyer."

"Why would you tell him that, Sara? You damn well knew I didn't have the package!"

"Yes, I know, but I really needed your help and that was the only way I could think of to get you there. I did not want you to be able to deliver the package. That is why I did not give you the location change."

"Exactly, what kind of game are you running, Sara?"

"Game, well the game is over, almost."

"I'm still not clear on what it is you are trying to tell me, Sara."

"Okay, I took the package from you the other day in the alley, right?"

"Yes, you did and why did you take my gun?"

"You were unconscious, and I did not want it to fall into the wrong hands. Maybe someone would have taken it, and used it in a crime or something, so I took it. Then I walked back to the apartment, I stashed the package and the gun in the apartment. Then I headed to their new location to put my plan into action. I figured if they didn't just shoot me then and there, I would have a chance to finish the job."

"Finish the job, wasn't the job getting the package?"

"Yes, but only as a piece of the whole. The whole job was getting the package and getting rid of the captain and his crew. That is why I brought the package here. I knew if I could get him up here to give him the package, I would be able to kill him and get rid of his men."

"Why didn't you let me know any of this?"

"I couldn't tell you; part of the deal was to implement this very covertly. It was on a need-to-know basis only, you understand, right?"

"Yes, I understand, so what now? The captain and his crew are gone."

"Ricky, we still have the package, right?"

"Yes, I have it well hidden. A lot of good that thing does us now."

"Could you, get it for me?"

"Sure, why do you want it?"

"No reason really, I just want to see the little package that caused so much trouble."

"Now hold on a minute, Sara, you told me you were flipped, you are with them now. So, if you ask me about some package, I will tell you I don't know anything."

"Okay, Ricky, listen to me, please. We said we were going to do this job, get paid, and be done with all this. Maybe we would collect two million dollars. Maybe we would be dead. I made a better deal; I made us a better deal. Actually, I was working a side deal at first—"

"Whoa, hold on, wait a second here, you were working a side deal?"

"Well, yes, after you told me that Yurjinsky's payoff could possibly be in bullets, I thought I would find another deal. Before any exchange took place there was a meeting. Two young Middle Eastern men met with me at a small Italian restaurant downtown. We had cocktails and talked for a while about the arrangements. They looked at each other and spoke quietly then they turned to me and offered to pay one million dollars for the package. I told them the price was three million dollars. They looked at each other, laughed, and left the meeting. It worked out though because a better deal was offered and I agreed to it."

"A deal, you made a deal for us without telling me? I did not flip, Sara, you did."

"Yes, I did, stop, and just listen. I will tell you the deal that I made. If you do not like the deal, you will be free to continue on whatever path you choose, fair enough?"

"Okay, Sara, so tell me, what kind of deal?"

"The deal went like this. I had to secure the package and eliminate Yurjinsky."

"Yes, you already told me that."

"What I did not get a chance to tell you is this. In exchange for the package and taking out Yurjinsky, you would agree to flip and quit."

"I would agree to flip, no, Sara, not me."

"If you do, we will receive complete amnesty for any wrongdoings, and we will receive four million dollars in cash. So, are you in or are you out?"

"What happens if I refuse to flip, Sara?"

"If you refuse, they will arrest you. You go down for espionage and the theft of top-secret data. You will be tried as a spy against the United States government."

"You will be sent to federal prison with no chance of parole."

"Is that all?"

"Yes, that pretty much sums it up. Oh, Ricky, they will also seize all of your personal holdings."

"So, in essence, Sara, this was a four-million-dollar contract on the captain."

"Yes, a four-million-dollar contract to eliminate the captain, and his men, and not to sell the package to a foreign power, returning it to them."

"I'm thinking I'm in, but how do I know you are not making this up? I mean you have done it before. Why should I believe you now?"

"Okay, fine, excuse me. I'm going to make a call."

"A call, who are you calling?"

"Just relax, Ricky, it is fine, really."

He goes into the bedroom and he grabs a weapon. He sticks it under his belt and covers it with the un-tucked tails of his dark blue dress shirt. He comes back into the living room. There is a knock on the door. He is very unsure about what is taking place right now and he is a little on edge. Sara opens the door, and it is Al and Alice. She invites them in. Ricky relaxes a bit, not sure why they were there. They all sit down on the sofa. Sara gets them all some drinks. She sits down on the sofa with them and begins talking with them about the events that had taken place. Ricky looks on and has no idea why she telling them all of this, he just listens. Sara finishes filling them in on everything that took place. Al gets up, Ricky watches him closely.

Al tells them, "I need to go get something, would you please excuse me?"

"Yes, sure Al," Sara says. Ricky sits back into the sofa while Sara and Alice engage in light conversation about Alice's fashion business. Al returns a few minutes later and he is carrying a brown leather briefcase.

He looks at Alice then at Sara. "Are we ready to finish this?"

Sara nods, Ricky sits up. Al places the briefcase on the sofa. As he leans over to open it, Ricky reaches for his gun. Al opens the case and slowly turns it toward Sara and Ricky. Al looks at Sara. "We knew about your meeting downtown. I'm curious, Sara, why didn't you do business with them? We know they finally offered almost the same payment amount, why is it you didn't take that deal?"

"You are correct, Al. Their offer was good, yes, but yours included something they could not offer."

"Okay then, this is what we agreed to, isn't it, Sara, four million dollars, in cash?"

"Yes, Al, that was part of the agreement, but what about the papers?"

"Well, what about the package?"

Ricky is shocked at what he is witnessing and thinking to himself, *four million dollars in cash in a fine brown leather briefcase from Al? What does Al, bowtie Al know, about the package? Where did Al the CPA get four million dollars? And what are these papers Sara is referring to?*

Sara looks at Ricky, passionately yet sternly, and states, "We really need the package."

He looks at her not sure if he should get it. Alice opens her bag and reaches into it. Ricky again puts his hand on his gun. Alice pulls out a large, orange-colored envelope. She opens it, reaches in, and carefully takes out a couple of documents. She looks them over then hands the papers to Sara. There were two documents; they were the amnesty documents, signed and raised stamped. There was one for Sara and one for Ricky.

"Now," Alice tells Sara, "We have shown you ours, now show us yours."

Sara again looks at Ricky; Ricky looks at Al.

"You mean you guys are *Feds?"*

They take out their I.D.s, Federal Bureau of Investigation. Ricky thinks to himself; *that's why I froze at Al's question in the piano bar. Everything else he said had a kind of Midwestern feel to the way he said it, except for that one question. When he asked me; where are you from, originally Ricky? That was pure New York. I froze because I couldn't figure it just then, so I had to get out of there.*

"Hello, Ricky, I am agent Michael Warren and this is Agent Cathy Johnson. Now, we have done what we said we were going to do. May we have the package please?"

Ricky gets up slowly, tightly clutching his amnesty document in his left hand. He goes into the kitchen. He feels around inside the cabinet and finds the package. He brings it into the living room. He looks at Sara, she nods and he warily hands the package over to Al. Al in turn hands the package over to Alice and she places it in her bag. Then Al closes the briefcase and slides it over to Sara. They say their goodbyes and they leave.

Ricky looks at Sara in disbelief, "Al and Alice, this whole time, feds?"

"Yes Ricky, the only people that did not know was Captain Yurjinsky, his men, John Klegman, and you."

"Why didn't you tell me? We went into their apartment; I took the codes from his machine. I set up feds as decoys!"

"Yes," she laughs, "yes, you sure did. They were on to it from the beginning."

"They knew?"

"John told me I was being played."

"He was correct, you were being played but not in the usual way."

"How did they know?"

"Well, one thing I found out is that you are not the only one with small wireless surveillance cameras."

"What are you saying?"

"I am saying that when we went into their apartment to 'water their plants,' we were being watched."

"Why didn't they do something to stop us if they knew?"

"Ricky, listen, it was all part of the setup. We set out to use them, right?"

"Yes."

"Well, they ended up using us. Do you remember their little getaway for a few days and then giving us a key to their apartment to water their plants? I didn't know then either. It was all part of their game to get to Yurjinsky. They used us to get the captain. They, uh, they also found out about John."

"What, how?"

"Did you give him up too?"

"No, surveillance cameras on site caught him throwing something over the fence."

"Wait a minute, there were no cameras that covered that area according to John."

"John was right. Normally there would have been no cameras in place for that area. They installed new HD cameras to observe the site walk-through for additional security. They caught everything you did during the walk-through. They even have you walking into a section that was off-limits. In addition, they caught you taking pictures with your phone."

"When the security team was viewing replays, they saw someone throwing something over the fence. When they digitally enlarged and enhanced the video image, they saw it was John. He had a package in his hand and is seen throwing it over the fence. The officials were called in. The officials went to his room with a security team. The security team seized his computer and brought it to the IT department. The IT analysts found the misappropriated secret data files. That is when they learned exactly what had been stolen and that is when Al and Alice approached me. They knew there would be many interested buyers."

"Why didn't they just go get it?"

"They needed to let it play out in order to get to the captain and get rid of him."

"It almost didn't play out, Sara. If Yurjinsky's Death Squad boys would have been successful, he would have had the package and been long gone. What's going to happen to John?"

"He's going to Federal prison with no chance of parole. Remember the end game was not just the package. It was the captain, his men, and the package. Everything that took place was done for that one outcome. The watchers across the street, the change in surveillance all staged to allow us to pull this off. They knew we were here and they knew we had met with the captain at Chelsea Pier but they didn't know why or what we were after."

"How did they know we met with the captain?"

"They were tailing him, not us. We just were caught with him from their photograph surveillance. They identified us, located our address, and set up across the street."

"That is why they had all of their surveillance watching us. They were anticipating maybe the captain, would show up here. When he arrived here with us, they had to wait for us, uh me, to carry out the plan. They wanted to be sure to get both the package and the captain. They set up Al and Alice one floor below to get acquainted and become friendly with us on purpose. The real tenants, the Elliston's, have been on an all-expenses-paid vacation enjoying luxury resort hotels in Europe."

"Well, there you have it. We now have complete amnesty, we are out of the game clean and we have four million dollars in cash, what do want to do first?"

"I think after all this *we* should go on a nice long vacation. What to do you say to that, Mrs. Rogers?"

"I say, yes! Yes to going on vacation and yes to being Mrs. Rogers."

Ricky calls their travel agent and books a trip to Tahiti. They reserve a suite at the simply beautiful Tahiti Pearl Beach Resort. While they were there, they had a small private nuptial ceremony on the beach to become officially Mr. and Mrs. Rogers. After the ceremony, they went down to the beach area where there are rows of thickly padded chaise lounges. They sit on the lounges set in the sand and watch the waves.

A waiter comes over to them, "Excuse me, I am Peter, would the gentleman and lady care for a cool refreshing beverage?"

"Hello Peter, yes that sounds great. Please bring us two frozen mango daiquiris."

"Yes sir, right away, sir."

Peter soon returns with their drinks. "Excuse me, sir?"

"Yes Peter, what do you need?"

"Sir, my manager said to give you the beverages at no charge; he said to tell you congratulations."

"Hey, Peter, that's great, please tell him thank you from us for his gift."

Peter turns to leave and Ricky calls out, "Peter, wait a minute, here, this is for you."

He hands Peter very generous gratuity. Peter looks at what he was given, and thanks them both very much. He heads back to the beach bar. Whistling on his way, to happily assist other guests of the resort beach bar. Ricky and Sara sit back and kind of sink into the deep, plush cushions on the chaise lounges. They relax and enjoy their drinks. The surf was still strong with serious 8 to 12-foot waves.

They were breaking out away from the shore on a coral reef. They watched the surf and half-dug their feet into the white sand, enjoying the serene scene that is Tahiti. After a while of tranquil silence, and just as the sun starts to set, he looks over at her and raises his glass.

"You pulled off an amazing deal, Mrs. Rogers, an absolutely amazing deal."

She looks at him, shows him the ring, smiles, and with the last traces of sunlight passing through her dark red hair, she looks at him. "Thank you, Mr. Rogers, I appreciate that."

She leans over and kisses him. They finish their drinks, get up, and walk to their room. They shower off the sand from the beach. After their showers, Sara fixes them a couple of cocktails. Ricky puts on some music, jazz of course. When they finish their drinks, they get up and go into the bedroom. He smiles at Sara as she slips off her robe and slides into bed between the ivory-colored satin sheets. He smiles at her, "Mission accomplished."

"No, we are not done yet, Mr. Rogers."

"No Mrs. Rogers?"

"No, it will not be 'mission accomplished' until you get into this bed with me."

And then…the lights go…*out.*

The End